THE PROVOST

JOHN GALT was born in Irvine, Ayrshire, in 1779 and was trained for business. At the age of twenty-four he moved to London. He was by turns continental traveller (for a time the companion of Byron), businessman in a variety of ventures, parliamentary lobbyist, colonial administrator in Canada (where his family ultimately settled), and, at all times, an indefatigable writer. He was the author of over forty books but his literary reputation was established and remains based on a series of Tales of the West, novels drawing on his memories of the Glasgow and Ayrshire region in which he grew up. His *Annals of the Parish* (1821), *The Provost* (1822), and *The Entail* (1822) are deeply felt studies of small-town life in eighteenth-century Scotland. He moved, with no great success, to historical fiction and in 1832 produced *The Member*, the first political novel in English. Though an invalid in his later years, he continued to write, and published a series of novellas. He died in 1839.

IAN A. GORDON is Emeritus Professor of English in the University of Wellington, New Zealand. He has edited several of Galt's novels and written a biography. Among his other books are *John Skelton*, *Katherine Mansfield*, *Shenstone's Miscellany*, *A Word in Your Ear*, and *The Movement of English Prose*.

THE WORLD'S CLASSICS

===

JOHN GALT

The Provost

===

Edited with an Introduction by
IAN A. GORDON

Oxford   New York
OXFORD UNIVERSITY PRESS
1982

Oxford University Press, Walton Street, Oxford OX2 6DP

London Glasgow New York Toronto
Delhi Bombay Calcutta Madras Karachi
Kuala Lumpur Singapore Hong Kong Tokyo
Nairobi Dar es Salaam Cape Town
Melbourne Auckland
and associates in
Beirut Berlin Ibadan Mexico City Nicosia

Introduction, Notes, Bibliography, and Chronology
© *Oxford University Press 1973, 1982*

First published 1973 by Oxford University Press
First issued as a World's Classics paperback 1982

British Library Cataloguing in Publication Data
Galt, John
The provost.—(The World's classics)
I. Title II. Gordon, Ian A.
823'.7 [F] PR4708.G2
ISBN 0-19-281629-2

Printed in Great Britain by
Hazell Watson & Viney Limited
Aylesbury, Bucks

CONTENTS

ACKNOWLEDGEMENTS

THE Galt-Blackwood letters cited in this edition are excerpted from the Blackwood papers in the National Library of Scotland (cited by NLS MS. number) and the early Letter Books (cited as LB 1–4) of William Blackwood and Sons, Edinburgh, by courtesy of the National Library of Scotland and the present head of the firm, G. D. Blackwood, Esq. For permission to inspect and cite the early Minute Books of 'the Provost's' Town Council I am indebted to the Town Clerk of the Royal Burgh of Irvine. The University of Wellington and the Carnegie Trust for the Universities of Scotland provided time and a grant-in-aid towards the travel involved in the research.

INTRODUCTION

I

THE PROVOST, first published in May 1822, was the fifth in the sequence of six Scottish regional stories that Galt wrote for William Blackwood between February 1820, when he submitted *The Ayrshire Legatees* to *Blackwood's Magazine*, and December 1822, when he published *The Entail*.[1] During these three years, Galt, hitherto known only as an industrious writer of travel-books, biographies, periodical articles, and numerous school text-books, emerged as a novelist of original powers. Full public recognition of his new status came with the appearance in May 1821 of *Annals of the Parish*, which aroused a chorus of praise from the critical periodicals and over night established his reputation.[2] Galt in later years was to claim that what he had created were not 'novels' but 'theoretical histories of society, limited, though they were required by the subject, necessarily to the events of a circumscribed locality'.[3] He had no need to be diffident. His achievement in the *Annals* and the sequence of studies of Scottish small-town life had been to expand the whole scope of the English novel.

By the time the *Annals* appeared in May 1821, Galt (who was living in London) had thrown himself into a group of new projects for Blackwood. *The Steamboat* was appearing monthly in the magazine; the composition of *Sir Andrew Wylie* advanced steadily; and, as if this were not enough, Galt proposed to Blackwood a plan for a 'citizen chronicle' parallel to the parish minister's 'Chronicle of Dalmailing' in the *Annals*. Blackwood replied on 20 May, 'I am quite delighted

[1] For fuller details of the planning and composition of the sequence, see my O.E.N. edition of *The Entail*, 1970, Introduction, pp. vii–xiii.

[2] In this series, ed. James Kinsley, 1967.

[3] *Autobiography*, 1833, ii, 220.

with the idea of Provost Hookie. It is a glorious subject',[1] and Galt was able to reassure him on 28 May that 'The provost is in a thriving way'.[2] During the summer of 1821 Galt worked steadily on all three projects. He moved to Edinburgh from September till January 1822 to complete *Sir Andrew Wylie*, suspending *The Provost* temporarily; but he took the opportunity to have a contract drawn up on 29 December, accepting 'One hundred Guineas for the copyright of the Provost to make a similar volume to the Annals of the Parish'.[3]

On his return to London, he reported on 13 February 1822 that he was 'going on with the provost'[4] and on 19 February sent a 'portion' with a request for 'two copies of the proofs'.[5] Further 'portions' followed in rapid succession and Blackwood was able to announce in the March number of his magazine a publication date 'early in May' and to insert in the London weekly *John Bull* of 24 March an advertisement stating that *The Provost* was 'in the press'. Blackwood continued to be delighted with each portion as it arrived in Edinburgh and, for once, refrained from his customary temptation to edit and amend. He had earlier incurred Galt's mild displeasure by 'pruning' manuscripts submitted and was later to provoke an angry reaction against wholesale 'interference'. But *The Provost* he accepted without pressing for alterations—'I have read again what you sent me—it is excellent',[6] he wrote of one portion, and, of another, 'I like it very much'.[7]

The entire manuscript was in his hands by April and, deserting his usual Edinburgh printers, he had the work set up by A. and R. Spottiswoode in London. Galt was able to keep a careful eye on the proofs—'I am quite sensible of a

[1] Blackwood to Galt. LB 2, f. 32. Blackwood's clerk misread 'Pawkie' as 'Hookie'.
[2] Galt to Blackwood. NLS MS. 4006, f. 235.
[3] Galt to Blackwood. NLS MS. 4006, f. 246.
[4] Galt to Blackwood. NLS MS. 4008, f. 160.
[5] Galt to Blackwood. NLS MS. 4008, f. 162.
[6] Blackwood to Galt, 5 March 1822. LB 2, f. 296.
[7] Blackwood to Galt, 23 March 1822. LB 2, f. 304.

manifest advantage in having the sheets before me as I correct, chiefly with a view to verbal repetitions—The eye catches things of that sort so much quicker in print than in MS'.[1] Blackwood's lack of editorial interference and the decision to print in London had two consequences, important for later readers. *The Provost* is the only Galt novel published by Blackwood which appeared precisely in the form intended by the author; and Galt's close supervision of the proofs resulted in an accurate text with which he was completely satisfied. It is, in particular, *the* authority for Galt's manner of handling the printing of dialect, the spelling and accidentals of which he supervised with meticulous care. This book always remained the novel in which he took most pride—'I, very simply perhaps, acknowledge, that to myself it has always appeared superior to the Annals of the Parish, to which work it was written as a companion.'[2]

The Provost was published in an edition of 2,000 in May. It was an immediate success. The June number of *Blackwood's Magazine* was able to report that the 2,000 copies had sold in a fortnight and a second edition of the same size was melting away 'like snaw aff a dyke'. Though there were some grumbles about Galt's 'powers of fertility' (the *Monthly Review* in May) the general tone of contemporary reviews was enthusiastic. The London *Literary Gazette* of 22 June gave *The Provost* a six-column review, significantly headed 'Mr. Galt's Novels', and made it the opportunity for a full-scale appreciation of an author 'deservedly held in very high estimation' who was 'like one of the Flemish masters'. The reputation established by *Annals of the Parish* was firmly—and finally—consolidated by *The Provost*.

---

[1] Galt to Blackwood, 'April 1822'. NLS MS. 4008, f. 171.
[2] *Literary Life*, 1834, i, 232.

2

The Provost is a brilliant fusion of two elements. The first is the small-town Scottish scene, which Galt had already exploited, most notably in the *Annals*. The second is the world of political action, which he had already handled with skill in the latter part of *Sir Andrew Wylie*. Galt, ever since as a young man he discovered Machiavelli, had been fascinated by the shrewd exercise of political power. As a political agent in London, lobbying in the House of Commons, he had seen it at work. His birthplace, the self-governing Royal Burgh of Irvine—the 'Gudetown' of *The Provost*—was large enough for political action, small enough to be displayed as a microcosm of the greater world beyond. Galt had left Irvine as a boy of ten; but he still retained a remarkably sharp memory of what he had heard discussed among his elders of the political manœuvres on the Town Council, the local gossip—in a burgh of a few thousand inhabitants—of who had bribed whom with cash or office, who had used his position for personal gain, who had contrived to secure for a friend an advantageous lease (or 'tack') of a piece of town property. He remembered an impressive, middle-aged Bailie Fullerton, fifty years a Town Councillor, three times Provost. By 1821 he must be long dead. He would form a convenient starting-point for a self-revealing and ironical portrait of 'Mr. Pawkie', a small-town politician.[1]

The 'period' of *The Provost* is the 'period' of the *Annals*, from 1760 to the 1820s. The scene is Scotland before the Industrial Revolution, a country waking from a long rural

[1] But 'Mr. Pawkie', by a supreme ironical twist, contrived to have the last word. Bailie Fullerton was not dead. On 16 September 1825 the nonagenarian Bailie signed the Town Council minutes, confirming that he had conferred the freedom of the Royal Burgh of Irvine on 'John Galt Esquire now of the City of London'. Galt recorded the incident in his *Literary Life*, 1834, i, 233–4, and said of his speech 'Provost Pawkie himself could never have said anything half so good'.

sleep to the promise of industry and commerce. The Reform Act had not been dreamt of. The Town Councils of the self-governing Scottish burghs were still, as they had been for centuries, self-perpetuating corporations. When a member died or retired, there was no election in the modern sense. The remaining members of a small Town Council picked a suitable successor. The town dignitaries were chosen in the same manner from within the limited group. The situation described in a report of 29 June 1710 by the Town Clerk of the Royal Burgh of Irvine was essentially unchanged during the sixty-year span of *The Provost*:

Their councill consists of fifteen merchants, including the provost, two baillies, dean of gild, and treasurer, and two trades, making in all seventeen. They elect their magistrats, viz., the provost and tuo baillies, yearly, the first Munday after Michalmass; and the Friday proceeding they leit [i.e. list] the magistrats, and do put tuo on the leit to the old provost and four to the tuo old baillies, and the Friday preceeding that they elect their new councill, and on the Friday after the election of the magistrats they choose their dean of gild, treasurer, clerk, fiscall, officers, visitors of mercats, birlamen [petty officers] etc. and are yearly obliged to change tuo merchants and tuo trades. And the provost and tuo baillies are not to continue above tuo years.[1]

Even the provisions about compulsory changes could be easily circumvented and—as *The Provost* shows—a determined manipulator could make the system work very nicely to his advantage whether he was formally in office or not. He could work his way, in this closed circle, up the hierarchy from Councillor to Provost, step aside (sure of re-election), retreat (*pour mieux sauter*), and learn—as Mr. Pawkie did—to make the Council do his will.

The Provost is a remarkable piece of writing. It has the photographic sharpness of Defoe. Everything is seen in clear detail. The topography of Gudetown is even today the recog-

---

[1] *Muniments of the Royal Burgh of Irvine*, Edinburgh, 1890–1, ii, 131.

nizable topography of Irvine. The events described can be (and are in the Explanatory Notes to this edition) documented from the early Minute Books of the Town Council. The progress of Mr. Pawkie is organized on a rigid time-scale that matches at every point the 'real' events of the time. In a sense, nothing is invented. Yet the whole novel is a considerable piece of imaginative creation, unified by Galt's ironical portrayal of the central figure.

James Pawkie recounts his career in town politics over the same years as Dr. Balwhidder's incumbency of the parish of Dalmailing. Galt chronicles the progress of a small Scottish town from 1760 to the early nineteenth century from the point of view of a sly ('pawkie') merchant who progresses from his apprenticeship, to his own shop, and then ownership of a considerable portion of the town (which he consumes like a 'caterpillar'), from a seat on the Town Council, where he soon learns 'to rule without being felt, which is the great mystery of policy', to the lucrative office of Dean of Guild, to Bailie, and finally to the supreme office of Provost, to which he contrives to be three times elected at strategic intervals, ensuring that both in office and in the intervening periods 'I was enabled to wind the council round my finger'.

Of all Galt's theoretical histories, *The Provost* is the most tightly constructed. There are no loose ends, no digressions, no alien interpolated passages. The self-told, self-revealing narrative moves steadily from young Pawkie's prudent choice of a profitable trade right to his masterly organizing as an old man of the vote of thanks and the 'very handsome silver cup, bearing an inscription in the Latin tongue', with which the council rewarded his service to Gudetown. He manipulates everybody and everything, the council, the corps of volunteers, the gentry, the local Member of Parliament, the newspaper, the traffic and the progress of the town. He can be kind; he is never ruthless. With grave decorum he feathers his own nest: public contracts contrive to effect improvements on or near his own properties; it is his shop that provides the uniforms for the volunteers—'I must confess', he writes, 'with a sort of sinister respect for my own interest'. But as he grows older (and wealthier) he 'had less incitement to be so grippy', and with a clear conscience he can become a reformer and can move (and insist on others moving) 'to partake of the purer spirit which the great mutations of the age had conjured into public affairs'. Galt's irony never falters.

3

The initial immediate success of *The Provost* was unquestionably due to its being accepted as a work of rich comedy. Its permanent value lies not so much in the succession of comic scenes as in Galt's subtle and ironic study in self-revelation. It is comedy with serious overtones not recognized by many of his early readers, who mainly saw in it a further instalment of Scots dialect humour. But, though Galt was unaware of it, the best critic of his age had bought *The Provost* and immediately recognized it as a masterpiece. Coleridge's copy came to light some years ago.[1] His annotation is—as usual—magistral and (with its side-glance at Wordsworth) can stand as the ultimate judgement on *The Provost*:

This work is not for the Many; but in the unconscious, perfectly natural, Irony of Self-delusion, in all parts intelligible to the intelligent Reader, without the slightest suspicion on the part of the Autobiographer, I know of no equal in our Literature. The governing Trait in the Provost's character is no where caricatured. In the character of Betty, John's wife, or the Beggar Girl intense Selfishness without malignity, as a *Nature*, and with all the innocence of a Nature, is admirably pourtrayed. In the Provost a similar *Selfness* is united with a *Slyness* and a plausibility eminently successful in cheating the man himself into a happy state of constant Self-applause. This and 'The Entail' would alone suffice to place Galt in the first rank of contemporary Novellists—and second only to Sir W. Scott in technique.

[1] See A. J. Ashley, 'Coleridge on Galt', *Times Literary Supplement*, 25 Sept. 1930, p. 757.

NOTE ON THE TEXT

THE text is printed from the Bodleian copy of the first edition, published in May 1822. Another edition, with the words 'Second Edition' on the title-page, appeared in June 1822. Comparison of the two editions with a Hinman collator reveals that, apart from the insertion of the words 'Second Edition' on the June title-page, the two are identical and from the same setting of type. A. and R. Spottiswoode, the printers, either held the type standing; or (as is more probable) shrewdly estimating Galt's popularity ran off a reserve of extra copies, which they bound up with a revised title-page. This would explain the speed with which the second edition was available.

A few minor misprints (involving broken or missing letters, hyphen errors, and a duplicated word) have been silently corrected. Otherwise the text is an exact reprint of the first edition, since *The Provost* (see Introduction) was proofed by Galt with great care.

SELECT BIBLIOGRAPHY

TWO editions (May and June, 1822) of *The Provost* appeared in Galt's lifetime. It was reprinted, with a modified text, with *The Steam Boat* and *The Omen* in Blackwood's Standard Novels, D. M. Moir being the editor (1841). This latter volume was re-issued in 1850 and 1869. An illustrated edition was issued in 1913 by T. N. Foulis, London and Edinburgh, and was reprinted (without the illustrations) in 1968 by C. Chivers, Ltd., Bath 'at the request of the Library Association'.

COLLECTED EDITIONS (MAIN NOVELS ONLY). *The Works of John Galt*, ed. D. S. Meldrum, introductions by S. R. Crockett, illustr., 8 vols. (Blackwood, 1895); *The Works of John Galt*, ed. D. S. Meldrum and W. Roughead, introductions by S. R. Crockett, illustr., 10 vols. (John Grant, 1936).

BIBLIOGRAPHY. Harry Lumsden, *The Bibliography of John Galt*, Records of the Glasgow Bibliographical Society (ix), 1931; B. A. Booth in the *Bulletin of Bibliography* (xvi), 1936. See also the books by R. K. Gordon, J. W. Aberdein, Ian Jack, and Ian A. Gordon noted below; and Lucien Leclaire, *A General Analytical Bibliography of the Regional Novelists of the British Isles 1800–1950* (Paris, 1954), pp. 31–5.

BIOGRAPHY AND CRITICISM. The primary sources are Galt's *Auto-biography*, 2 vols. (1833), and his *Literary Life, and Miscellanies*, 3 vols. (1834). The earliest memoir is by '∆' (D. M. Moir) in the 1841 edition of the *Annals*; modern biographies by J. W. Aberdein (1936), Ian A. Gordon (1972). For early criticism see *Blackwood's Magazine*, June 1822 (on his Scottish works prior to *The Entail*); *The Literary Gazette* (London), June 1822; *Edinburgh Review*, October 1923 ('Secondary Scottish Novels').

Modern Studies: J. H. Millar, literary *History of Scotland* (1903); R. K. Gordon, *John Galt* (Toronto, 1920); G. Kitchin in *Edinburgh Essays on Scots literature*, ed. H. J. C. Grierson (1933); J. W. Aberdein, *John Galt* (1936); F. H. Lyell, *A Study of the Novels of John Galt*, 1942 (Princeton Studies in English, no. 28); Lucien Leclaire, *Le Roman régionaliste dans les Iles Britanniques 1800–1950* (Paris, 1954); W. Croft Dickinson, *John Galt, 'The Provost' and the Burgh* (Greenock, 1954); Erik Frykman, *John Galt's*

Scottish Stories 1820–1823 (Uppsala, 1959); David Craig, *Scottish Literature and the Scottish People 1830–1860* (1961); Ian Jack, *English Literature 1815–1832* (1963), ch. viii; W. M. Parker, *Susan Ferrier and John Galt* (1965); K. M. Costain, 'The Prince and The Provost', *Studies in Scottish literature*, July 1968; Marion Lochhead, 'John Galt', *Maga*, December 1968; Ian A. Gordon, *John Galt, The Life of a Writer*, 1972.

A CHRONOLOGY OF JOHN GALT

THE PROVOST

INTRODUCTION

DURING a recent visit to the West Country, among other old friends, we paid our respects to Mrs. Pawkie, the relict of the Provost of that name, who three several times enjoyed the honour of being chief magistrate in Gudetown.[1] Since the death of her worthy husband, and the comfortable settlement in life of her youngest daughter, Miss Jenny, who was married last year, to Mr. Caption, Writer to the Signet,[2] she has been, as she told us herself, 'beeking in the lown[3] o' the conquest which the gudeman had, wi sic an ettling[4] o' pains and industry, gathered for his family.'

Our conversation naturally diverged into various topics, and, among others, we discoursed at large on the manifold improvements which had taken place, both in town and country, since we had visited the Royal Borough. This led the widow, in a complimentary way, to advert to the hand which, it is alleged, we have had in the editing of that most excellent work, entitled, 'Annals of the Parish of Dalmailing,' intimating, that she had a book in the hand-writing of her deceased husband, the Provost, filled with a variety of most curious matter; in her opinion, of far more consequence to the world, than any book that we had ever been concerned in putting out.

Considering the veneration in which Mr. Pawkie had been through life regarded by his helpmate, we must confess, that her eulogium on the merits of his work did not impress us with the most profound persuasion that it was really deserving of much attention. Politeness, however, obliged us to express an earnest desire to see the volume, which after some little hesitation was produced. Judge then of the nature of our emotions, when, in cursorily turning over a few of the well-penned pages, we found that it far surpassed every thing the lady had said in its praise. Such indeed was our surprise, that we could not refrain from openly and at once assuring her, that the delight and satisfaction which it was calculated to afford, rendered it a duty on her part to lose no time in submitting it to the public; and, after lavishing a panegyric on the singular and excellent qualities of the author, which was all most delicious to his widow, we concluded with a delicate insinuation of the pleasure we should enjoy, in being made the humble instrument of introducing to the knowledge of mankind a volume so replete and enriched with the fruits of his practical wisdom. Thus, partly by a judicious administration of flattery, and partly also by solicitation, backed by an indirect proposal to share the profits, we succeeded in persuading Mrs. Pawkie to allow us to take the valuable manuscript to Edinburgh, in order to prepare it for publication.

Having obtained possession of the volume, we lost no time, till we had made ourselves master of its contents. It appeared to consist of a series of detached notes, which, together, formed something analogous to an historical view of the different important and interesting scenes and affairs the Provost had been personally engaged in during his long magisterial life. We found, however, that the concatenation of the memoranda which he had made of public transactions, was in several places interrupted by the insertion of matter not in the least degree interesting to the nation at large; and that in arranging the work for the press, it would be requisite and proper to omit many of the notes and much of the record, in order to preserve the historical coherency of the narrative. But in doing this, the text has been retained inviolate, in so much, that while we congratulate the world on the addition we are thus enabled to make to the stock of public knowledge, we cannot but felicitate ourselves on the complete and consistent form into which we have so successfully reduced our precious materials; the separation of which, from the dross of personal and private anecdote, was a task of no small difficulty; such, indeed, as the Editors only of the autographic memoirs of other great men can duly appreciate.

CHAPTER I

THE FORECAST

IT must be allowed in the world, that a man who has thrice reached the highest station of life, in his line, has a good right to set forth the particulars of the discretion and prudence by which he lifted himself so far above the ordinaries of his day and generation; indeed, the generality of mankind may claim this as a duty; for the conduct of public men, as it has been often wisely said, is a species of public property, and their rules and observances have in all ages been considered things of a national concernment. I have therefore well weighed the importance it may be of to posterity, to know by what means I have thrice been made an instrument to represent the supreme power and authority of Majesty, in the royal borough of Gudetown, and how I deported myself in that honour and dignity, so much to the satisfaction of my superiors in the state and commonwealth of the land, to say little of the great respect in which I was held by the townsfolk, and far less of the terror that I was to evildoers. But not to be over circumstantial, I propose to confine this history of my life to the public portion thereof, on the which account I will take up the beginning at the crisis when I first entered into business, after having served more than a year above my time, with the late Mr. Thomas Remnant, than whom there was not a more creditable man in the borough; and he died in the possession of the functionaries and faculties of town Treasurer, much respected by all acquainted with his orderly and discreet qualities.

Mr. Remnant was, in his younger years, when the growth of luxury and prosperity had not come to such a head as it has done since, a taylor that went out to the houses of the adjacent lairds and country gentry, whereby he got an inkling of the policy of the world, that could not have been gathered in any other way by a man of his station and degree of life. In process of time he came to be in a settled way, and when I was bound 'prentice to him, he had three regular journeymen, and a cloth shop. It was therefore not so much for learning the tayloring, as to get an insight into the conformity between the traffic of the shop and the board[1] that I was bound to him, being destined by my parents for the profession appertaining to the former, and to conjoin thereto something of the mercery and haberdashery; my uncle, that had been a sutler in the army along with General Wolfe, who made a conquest of Quebec,[2] having left me a legacy of three hundred pounds, because I was called after him, the which legacy was a consideration for to set me up in due season in some genteel business.

Accordingly, as I have narrated, when I had passed a year over my 'prenticeship with Mr. Remnant, I took up the corner shop at the Cross, facing the Tolbooth,[3] and having had it adorned in a befitting manner, about a month before the summer fair thereafter, I opened it on that day, with an excellent assortment of goods, the best, both for taste and variety, that had ever been seen in the borough of Gudetown; and the winter following, finding by my books that I was in a way to do so, I married my wife: she was daughter to Mrs. Broderip, who kept the head inn in Irville,[4] and by whose death, in the fall of the next year, we got a nest egg, that, without a vain pretension, I may say we have not failed to lay upon, and clok[5] to some purpose.

Being thus settled in a shop and in life, I soon found that I had a part to perform in the public world; but I looked warily about me before casting my nets, and therefore I laid myself out, rather to be entreated than to ask; for I had often heard Mr. Remnant observe, that the nature of man could not abide to see a neighbour taking place and preferment of his own accord. I therefore assumed a coothy[6] and obliging demeanour towards my customers and the community in general; and sometimes even with the very beggars I found a jocose saying as well received as a bawbee,[1] although naturally I dinna think I was ever what could be called a funny man, but only just as ye would say a thought ajee[2] in that way. Howsever, I soon became, both by habit and repute, a man of popularity in the town, in so much, that it was a shrewd saying of old James Alpha, the bookseller, that 'mair gude jokes were cracked ilka day in James Pawkie's shop, than in Thomas Curl, the barber's, on a Saturday night.'

CHAPTER II

A KITHING[3]

I COULD plainly discern that the prudent conduct which I had adopted towards the public was gradually growing into effect. Disputative neighbours made me their referee, and I became, as it were, an oracle that was better than the law, in so much that I settled their controversies without the expence that attends the same. But what convinced me more than any other thing that the line I pursued was verging towards a satisfactory result, was, that the elderly folk that came into the shop to talk over the news of the day, and to rehearse the diverse uncos,[4] both of a national and a domestic nature, used to call me bailie, and my lord; the which jocular derision was as a symptom and foretaste within their spirits of what I was ordained to be. Thus was I encouraged, by little and little, together with a sharp remarking of the inclination and bent of men's minds, to entertain the hope and assurance of rising to the top of all the town, as this book maketh manifest, and the incidents thereof will certificate.

Nothing particular, however, came to pass till my wife lay in of her second bairn, our daughter Sarah; at the christening of whom, among divers friends and relations, forbye the minister, we had my father's cousin, Mr. Alexander Clues, that was then deacon Covener,[1] and a man of great potency in his way, and possessed of an influence in the town council, of which he was well worthy, being a person of good discernment, and well versed in matters appertaining to the guildry.[2] Mr. Clues, as we were mellowing over the toddy bowl, said, that by and by the council would be looking to me to fill up the first gap that might happen therein; and Doctor Swapkirk, the then minister, who had officiated on the occasion, observed, that it was a thing, that in the course of nature, could not miss to be, for I had all the douce demeanour and sagacity which it behoved a magistrate to possess. But I cannily[3] replied, though I was right contented to hear this, that I had no time for governing, and it would be more for the advantage of the commonwealth to look for the counselling of an older head than mine, happen when a vacancy might in the town council.

In this conjuncture of our discoursing, Mrs. Pawkie, my wife, who was sitting by the fire-side in her easy chair, with a cod[4] at her head, for she had what was called a sore time o't, said,

'Na, na, gudeman, ye need ne be sae mim[5]; every body kens, and I ken too, that ye're ettling at[6] the magistracy. Its as plain as a pike staff, gudeman, and I'll no let ye rest if ye dinna mak me a bailie's wife or a' be done—'

I was not ill pleased to hear Mrs. Pawkie so spiritful; but I replied, 'Dinna try to stretch your arm, gudewife, farther than your sleeve will let you; we maun ca' canny[7] mony a day yet, before we think of dignities.'

The which speech, in a way of implication, made deacon Clues to understand that I would not absolutely refuse an honour thrust upon me, while it maintained an outward show of humility and moderation.

There was, however, a gleg old carlin[8] among the gossips then present, one Mrs. Sprowl, the widow of a deceased magistrate, and she cried out aloud,

'Deacon Clues, deacon Clues, I redde[1] you no to believe a word that Mr. Pawkie's saying, for that was the very way my friend[2] that's no more laid himself out to be fleeched[3] to tak what he was greenan for;[4] so get him intill the council when ye can; we a' ken he'll be credit to the place,' and 'so here's to the health of Bailie Pawkie, that is to be,' cried Mrs. Sprowl. All present pledged her in the toast, by which we had a wonderful share of diversion. Nothing, however, immediately rose out of this, but it set men's minds a barming[5] and working, so that before there was any vacancy in the council, I was considered in a manner as the natural successor to the first of the counsellors that might happen to depart this life.

CHAPTER III

A DIRGIE[6]

IN the course of the summer following the baptism, of which I have rehearsed the particulars in the foregoing chapter, Bailie Mucklehose happened to die, and as he was a man long and well respected, he had a great funeral. All the rooms in his house were filled with the company; and it so fell out, that, in the confusion, there was neither minister nor elder to give the blessing sent into that wherein I was, by which, when Mr. Shavings, the wright, with his men, came in with the service of bread and wine, as usual, there was a demur, and one after another of those present was asked to say grace; but none of them being exercised in public prayer, all declined, when Mr. Shavings said to me, 'Mr. Pawkie, I hope ye'll no refuse.'

I had seen, in the process, that not a few of the declinations were more out of the awkward shame of blateness,[7] than any inherent modesty of nature, or diffidence of talent; so, without making a phrase about the matter, I said the grace, and in such a manner, that I could see it made an impression. Mr. Shavings was at that time deacon[1] of the wrights, and being well pleased with my conduct on this occasion, when he, the same night, met the craft, he spoke of it in a commendable manner, and as I understood thereafter, it was thought by them, that the council could not do better than make choice of me to the vacancy. In short, no to spin out the thread of my narration beyond necessity, let it here suffice to be known, that I was chosen into the council, partly by the strong handling of Deacon Shavings, and the instrumentality of other friends and well-wishers, and not a little by the moderation and prudence with which I had been secretly ettling at[2] the honour.

Having thus reached to a seat in the council, I discerned that it behoved me to act with circumspection, in order to gain a discreet dominion over the same, and to rule without being felt, which is the great mystery of policy. With this intent, I, for some time, took no active part in the deliberations, but listened, with the doors of my understanding set wide to the wall, and the windows of my foresight all open; so that, in process of time, I became acquainted with the inner man of the counsellors, and could make a guess no far short of the probability, as to what they would be at, when they were jooking and wising[3] in a round-about manner to accomplish their own several wills and purposes. I soon thereby discovered, that although it was the custom to deduce reasons from out the interests of the community, for the divers means and measures that they wanted to bring to a bearing for their own particular behoof, yet this was not often very cleverly done, and the cloven-foot of self-interest was now and then to be seen aneath the robe of public principle. I had, therefore, but a straight forward course to pursue, in order to overcome all their wiles and devices, the which was to make the interests of the community, in truth and sincerity, the end and object of my study, and never to step aside from it, for any immediate speciality of profit to myself. Upon this, I have endeavoured to walk with a constancy of sobriety; and, although I have, to a certainty, reaped advantage both in my own person and that of my family, no man living can accuse me of having bent any single thing pertaining to the town and public, from the natural uprightness of its integrity, in order to serve my own private ends.

It was, however, some time before an occasion came to pass, wherein I could bring my knowledge and observations to operate in any effectual manner towards a reformation in the management of the borough; indeed, I saw that no good could be done until I had subdued the two great factions, into which it may be said the council was then divided; the one party being strong for those of the king's government of ministers, and the other no less vehement on the side of their adversaries. I, therefore, without saying a syllable to any body anent the same, girded myself for the undertaking, and with an earnest spirit, put my shoulder to the wheel, and never desisted in my endeavours, till I had got the cart up the brae,[1] and the whole council reduced into a proper state of subjection to the will and pleasure of his majesty, whose deputies and agents I have ever considèred all inferior magistrates to be, administering and exercising, as they do, their power and authority in his royal name. The ways and means, however, by which this was brought to pass, supply matter for another chapter; and after this, it is not my intent to say any thing more concerning my principles and opinions, but only to show forth the course and current of things proceeding out of the affairs, in which I was so called to perform a part requiring no small endeavour and diligence.

CHAPTER IV

THE GUILDRY

WHEN, as is related in the foregoing chapter, I had nourished my knowledge of the council into maturity, I began to cast about for the means of exercising the same towards a satis-

factory issue. But in this I found a great difficulty, arising from
the policy and conduct of Mr. Andrew M'Lucre, who had a
sort of infœftment,[1] as may be said, of the office of Dean of
Guild,[2] having for many years been allowed to intromit[3] and
manage the same; by which, as was insinuated by his adversaries, no little grist came to his mill. For it had happened from
a very ancient date, as far back, I have heard, as the time of
Queen Anne, when the union of the kingdoms was brought to
a bearing, that the Dean of Guild among us, for some reason
or another, had the upper hand in the setting and granting of
tacks[4] of the town lands, in the doing of which it was jealoused[5]
that the predecessors of Mr. M'Lucre, no to say an ill word
of him, honest man, got their loofs creeshed[6] with something
that might be called a grassum,[7] or rather, a gratus gift. It
therefore seemed to me that there was a necessity for some
reformation in the office, and I foresaw that the same would
never be accomplished, unless I could get Mr. M'Lucre
wised[8] out of it, and myself appointed his successor. But in this
lay the obstacle, for every thing anent the office was, as it
were, in his custody, and it was well known that he had an
interest in keeping by that which, in vulgar parlance, is called
nine points of the law. However, both for the public good and
a convenience to myself, I was resolved to get a finger in the
Dean of Guild's fat pye, especially as I foresaw that, in the
course of three or four years, some of the best tacks would
run out, and it would be a great thing to the magistrate that
might have the disposal of the new ones. Therefore, without
seeming to have any foresight concerning the lands that were
coming on to be out of lease, I set myself to constrain Mr.
M'Lucre to give up the Guildry, as it were, of his own free
will; and what helped me well to this, was a rumour that came
down from London, that there was to be a dissolution of the
Parliament.

   The same day that this news reached the town, I was standing at my shop-door, between dinner and tea-time.[9] It was a
fine sunny summer afternoon. Standing under the blessed

influence of the time by myself at my shop-door, who should I see passing along the crown of the causey,[1] but Mr. M'Lucre himself, and with a countenance knotted with care, little in unison with the sultry indolence of that sunny day.

'Whar[2] awa sae fast, Dean o' Guild?' quo' I to him; and he stopped his wide stepping, for he was a long spare man, and looting[3] in his gait.

'I'm just,' said he, 'taking a step to the Provost's, to learn the particulars of thir[4] great news—for as we are to hae the casting vote in the next election,[5] there's no saying the good it may bring to us all, gin we manage it wi discretion.'

I reflected the while of a minute before I made any reply, and then I said—

'I would hae na doubt of the matter, Mr. M'Lucre, could it be brought about to get you chosen for the delegate; but I fear, as ye are only Dean of Guild this year, that's no to be accomplished; and really, without the like of you, our borough, in the contest, may be driven to the wall.'

'Contest!' cried the Dean of Guild, with great eagerness; 'wha told you that we are to be contested?'

Nobody had told me, nor at the moment was I sensible of the force of what I said; but seeing the effect it had on Mr. M'Lucre, I replied—

'It does not, perhaps, just now, do for me to be more particular, and I hope what I have said to you will gang no farther; but it's a great pity that ye're no even a bailie this year, far less the provost, otherwise I would have great confidence.'

'Then,' said the Dean of Guild, 'you have reason to believe that there is to be a dissolution, and that we are to be contested?'

'Mr. M'Lucre, dinna spear[6] any quistions,' was my answer, 'but look at that, and say nothing;' so I pulled out of my pocket a letter that had been franked to me by the Earl.[7] The letter was from James Portoport, his lordship's butler, who had been a waiter with Mrs. Pawkie's mother, and he was inclosing to me a five-pound note to be given to an auld aunty, that was in need. But the Dean of Guild knew nothing of our correspondence, nor was it required that he should. However, when he saw my Lord's franking, he said, 'Are the boroughs, then, really and truly to be contested?'

'Come into the shop, Mr. M'Lucre,' said I, sedately; 'come in, and hear what I have to say.'

And he came in, and I shut and barred the half-door,[1] in order that we might not be suddenly interrupted.

'You are a man of experience, Mr. M'Lucre,' said I, 'and have a knowledge of the world, that a young man, like me, would be a fool to pretend to. But I have shown you enough to convince you that I would not be worthy of a trust, were I to answer any improper questions. Ye maun, therefore, gie me some small credit for a little discretion in this matter, while I put a question to yourself.—Is there no a possibility of getting you made the provost at Michaelmas,[2] or, at the very least, a bailie, to the end that ye might be chosen delegate, it being an unusual thing for any body under the degree of a bailie to be chosen thereto?'

'I have been so long in the guildry,' was his thoughtful reply, 'that I fear it canna be very well managed without me.'

'Mr. M'Lucre,' said I, and I took him cordially by the hand, 'a thought has just entered my head. Could na we manage this matter between us? It's true I'm but a novice in public affairs, and with the mystery of the guildry quite unacquaint—if, however, you could be persuaded to allow yourself to be made a bailie, I would, subject to your directions, undertake the office of Dean of Guild, and all this might be so concerted between us, that nobody would ken the nature of our paction— for, to be plain with you, its no to be hoped that such a young counsellor as myself can reasonably expect to be raised, so soon as next Michaelmas, to the magistracy,[3] and there is not another in the council that I would like to see chosen delegate at the election but yourself.'

Mr. M'Lucre swithered[4] a little at this, fearing to part with the bird he had in hand; but, in the end, he said, that he thought what was proposed no out of the way, and that he would have no objection to be a bailie for the next year, on condition that I would, in the following, let him again be Dean of Guild, even though he should be called a Michaelmas mare,[1] for it did not so well suit him to be a bailie as to be Dean of Guild, in which capacity he had been long used.

I guessed in this that he had a vista in view of the tacks and leases that were belyve[2] to fall in, and I said,—

'Nothing can be more reasonable, Mr. M'Lucre; for the office of dean of guild must be a very fashious[3] one, to folks like me, no skilled in its particularities; and I'm sure I'll be right glad and willing to give it up, when we hae got our present turn served.—But to keep a' things quiet between us, let us no appear till after the election, overly thick; indeed, for a season, we maun fight, as it were, under different colours.'

Thus was the seed sown of a great reformation in the borough, the sprouting whereof I purpose to describe in due season.

CHAPTER V

THE FIRST CONTESTED ELECTION

THE sough[4] of the dissolution of parliament, during the whole of the summer, grew stronger and stronger, and Mr. M'Lucre and me were seemingly pulling at opposite ends of the rope. There was nothing that he proposed in the council but what I set myself against with such bir[5] and vigour, that sometimes he could scarcely keep his temper even while he was laughing in his sleeve to see how the other members of the corporation were beglammered. At length Michaelmas drew near, when I, to show as it were that no ill blood had been bred on my part, notwithstanding our bickerings, proposed in the council, that Mr. M'Lucre should be the new bailie, and he on his part to manifest, in return, that there was as little heart-burning on his, said 'he would have no objections; but then he insisted that I should consent to be Dean of Guild in his stead.'

'It's true,' said he in the council on that occasion, 'that Mr. Pawkie is as yet but a green-horn in the concerns of the borough; however, he'll never learn younger, and if he'll agree to this, I'll gie[1] him all the help and insight that my experience enables me to afford.'

At the first, I pretended that really, as was the truth, I had no knowledge of what were the duties of Dean of Guild; but after some fleeching[2] from the other councillors, I consented to have the office as it were forced upon me; so I was made Dean of Guild, and Mr. M'Lucre the new bailie.

By and bye, when the harvest in England was over, the parliament was dissolved, but no candidate started on my Lord's interest, as was expected by Mr. M'Lucre, and he began to fret and be dissatisfied that he had ever consented to allow himself to be hoodwinked out of the guildry. However, just three days before the election, and at the dead hour of the night, the sound of chariot wheels and of horsemen was heard in our streets, and this was Mr. Galore, the great Indian Nabob,[3] that had bought the Beerland estates, and built the grand place that is called Lucknoo-House, coming from London, with the influence of the crown on his side, to oppose the old member. He drove straight to Provost Picklan's house, having, as we afterwards found out, been in a secret correspondence with him through the medium of Mrs. Picklan, who was conjunct in the business with Miss Nelly, the Nabob's maiden sister. Mr. M'Lucre was not a little confounded at this, for he had imagined that I was the agent on behalf of my Lord, who was of the government side, so he wist not what to do, in the morning when he came to me, till I said to him briskly—

'Ye ken, Bailie, that ye're trysted to me, and it's our duty to support the nabob who is both able and willing, as I have good reason to think, to requite our services in a very grateful manner.' This was a cordial to his spirit, and, without more ado, we both of us set to work to get the bailie made the delegate. In this I had nothing in view but the good of my country by pleasuring, as it was my duty, his Majesty's government, for I was satisfied with my situation as Dean of Guild. But the handling required no small slight of skill.

The first thing was, to persuade those that were on the side of the old member to elect Mr. M'Lucre for delegate, he being, as we had concerted, openly declared for that interest, and the benefit to be gotten thereby having, by use and wont, been at an established and regular rate. The next thing was to get some of those that were with me on my Lord's side,[1] kept out of the way on the day of choosing the delegate; for we were the strongest, and could easily have returned the provost, but I had no clear notion how it would advantage me, to make the provost delegate as was proposed. I therefore, on the morning of the business, invited three of the council to take their breakfast with me for the ostensible purpose of going in a body to the council chamber to choose the provost delegate; but when we were at breakfast, John Snakers, my lad in the shop, by my suggestion, warily got a bale of broad cloth so tumbled as it were by accident at the door, that it could not be opened, for it bent the key in such a manner in the lock, and crooket the snek,[2] that without a smith there was no egress, and sorrow a smith was to be had. All were out and around the tolbooth waiting for the upshot of the choosing the delegate. Those that saw me in the meantime, would have thought I had gone demented: I ramped and I stamped, I banned[3] and I bellowed like desperation. My companions no a bit better, flew fluttering to the windows, like wild birds to the wires of their cage.—However, to make a long tale short, Bailie M'Lucre was by means of this device[4] chosen delegate, seemingly against my side.—But oh! he was a slee tod,[5] for no sooner was he so chosen, than he began to act for his own behoof, and that very afternoon, while both parties were holding their public dinner, he sent round the bell to tell that the potatoe

crop on his back rig¹ was to be sold by way of public roup²
the same day. There wasna one in the town that had reached
the years of discretion, but kent what na sort of potatoes he
was going to sell; and I was so disturbed by this open corruption, that I went to him, and expressed my great surprise. Hot
words ensued between us, and I told him very plainly that I
would have nothing further to say to him or his political
profligacy. However his potatoes were sold, and brought
upwards of three guineas the peck,³ the Nabob being the pur-
chaser, who, to show his contentment with the bargain, made
Mrs. M'Lucre, and the bailie's three daughters, presents of
new gowns and prin-cods,⁴ that were not stuffed with wool.

In the end, as a natural consequence, Bailie M'Lucre, as
delegate, voted for the Nabob, and the old member was
thereby thrown out. But although the government-candidate
in this manner won the day, yet I was so displeased by the
jookerie⁵ of the bailie, and the selfish manner by which he had
himself reaped all the advantage of the election in the sale of
his potatoes, that we had no correspondence on public affairs,
till long after; so that he never had the face to ask me to give
up the Guildry, till I resigned it of my own accord, after the
renewal of the tacks to which I have alluded, by the which
renewals, a great increase was effected in the income of the
town.

CHAPTER VI

THE FAILURE OF BAILIE M'LUCRE

Bailie M'Lucre, as I have already intimated, was
naturally a greedy bodie,⁶ and not being content with the
profits of his potatoe rig, soon after the election, he set up as
an o'er-sea merchant,⁷ buying beef and corn by agency in
Ireland, and having the same sent to the Glasgow market. For
some time, this traffic yielded him a surprising advantage; but

the summer does not endure the whole year round, nor was
his prosperity ordained to be of a continuance. One mishap
befel him after another; cargoes of his corn heated in the
vessels, because he would not sell at a losing price, and so
entirely perished; and merchants broke, that were in his debt
large sums for his beef and provisions. In short, in the course
of the third year from the time of the election, he was rookit of
every plack[1] he had in the world, and was obligated to take the
benefit of the divor's bill,[2] soon after which he went suddenly
away from the town, on the pretence of going into Edinburgh,
on some business of legality with his wife's brother, with
whom he had entered into a plea, concerning the moieté of a
steading[3] at the town-head.[4] But he did not stop on any such
concern there; on the contrary, he was off, and up to London
in a trader from Leith, to try if he could get a post in the
Government by the aid of the Nabob, our member; who, by
all accounts, was hand and glove with the King's ministers.
The upshot of this journey to London was very comical; and
when the bailie afterwards came back, and him and me were
again on terms of visitation, many a jocose night we spent over
the story of the same, for the bailie was a kittle hand at a bowl
of toddy; and his adventure was so droll, especially in the way
he was wont to rehearse the particulars, that it cannot fail to
be an edification to posterity, to read and hear how it happened, and all about it. I may therefore take leave to digress
into the circumstantials, by way of lightening for a time the
seriousness of the sober and important matter, whereof it is
my intent that this book shall be a register and record to future
times.

CHAPTER VII

THE BRIBE

MR. M'LUCRE, going to London, as I have intimated in the foregoing chapter, remained there, absent from us altogether about the space of six weeks; and when he came home, he was plainly an altered man, being sometimes very jocose, and at other times looking about him, as if he had been haunted by some ill-thing. Moreover, Mrs. Spell, that had the post-office from the decease of her husband, Deacon Spell, told among her kimmers,[1] that surely the bailie had a great correspondence with the King and Government, for that scarce a week passed without a letter from him to our member, or a letter from the member to him. This bred no small consideration among us; and I was somehow a thought uneasy thereat, not knowing what the bailie, now that he was out of the guildry, might be saying anent the use and wont that had been practiced therein, and never more than in his own time. At length, the babe was born.

One evening, as I was sitting at home, after closing the shop for the night, and conversing concerning the augmentation of our worldly affairs with Mrs. Pawkie and the bairns; it was a damp raw night; I mind it just as well as if it had been only yestreen; who should make his appearance at the room door but the bailie himself? and a blithe face he had.

'It's a' settled now,' cried he, as he entered with a triumphant voice; 'the siller's[2] my ain, and I can keep it in spite of them; I don't value them now a cutty-spoon[3]; no, not a doit; no the worth of that; nor a' their sprose[4] about New-gate and the pillory;'—and he snapped his fingers with an aspect of great courage.

'Hooly,[5] hooly, Bailie,' said I; 'what's a' this for;' and then he replied, taking his seat beside me at the fire-side—'The plea with the custom-house folk at London is settled, or rather, there canna be a plea at a', so firm and true is the laws of England on my side, and the liberty of the subject.'

All this was Greek and Hebrew to me, but it was plain, that the bailie, in his jaunt, had been guilty of some notour[1] thing, wherein the custom-house was concerned, and that he thought all the world was acquaint with the same. However, no to balk him in any communication he might be disposed to make to me, I said:—

'What ye say, Bailie, is great news, and I wish you meickle joy, for I have had my fears about your situation for some time; but now that the business is brought to such a happy end, I would like to hear all the true particulars of the case; and that your tale and tidings sha'na lack slockening,[2] I'll get in the toddy-bowl and the gardevin[3]; and with that, I winket to the mistress to take the bairns to their bed, and bade Jenny Hachle, that was then our feed servant lass, to gar[4] the kettle boil. Poor Jenny, has long since fallen into a great decay of circumstances, for she was not overly snod and cleanly in her service; and so, in time, wore out the endurance of all the houses and families that feed her, till nobody would take her; by which she was in a manner cast on Mrs. Pawkie's hands; who, on account of her kindliness towards the bairns in their childhood, has given her a howf[5] among us. But, to go on with what I was rehearsing; the toddy being ordered, and all things on the table, the bailie, when we were quiet by ourselves, began to say,—

'Ye ken weel, Mr. Pawkie, what I did at the lection for the member, and how angry ye were yoursel about it, and a' that. But ye were greatly mista'en, in thinking that I got ony effectual fee at the time, over and above the honest price of my potatoes; which ye were as free to bid for, had ye liket, as either o' the candidates. I'll no deny, however, that the Nabob, before he left the town, made some small presents to my wife and dochter; but that was no fault o' mine. Howsever, when a' was o'er, and I could discern, that ye were mindet to keep the guildry, I thought, after the wreck o' my provision concern, I might throw mair bread on the water and not find it, than by a bit jaunt to London to see how my honourable friend, the Nabob, was coming on in his place in Parliament, as I saw none of his speeches in the newspaper.

'Well, ye see, Mr. Pawkie, I gaed up to London in a trader from Leith; and by the use of a gude Scotch tongue, the whilk was the main substance o' a' the bairns' part o' geer[1] that I inherited from my parents, I found out the Nabob's dwelling, in the west end o' the town of London; and finding out the Nabob's dwelling, I went and rappit at the door, which a bardy[2] flunkie opened, and speer't[3] what I wantit, as if I was a thing no fit to be lifted off a midden with a pair of iron tongs. Like master, like man, thought I to myself; and, thereupon, taking heart no to be put out, I replied, to the whipper-snapper,—'I'm Bailie M'Lucre, o' Gudetown, and maun hae a word wi' his honour.

'The cur lowered his birsses[4] at this, and replied, in a mair ceeveleezed style of language, 'Master is not at home.' But I kent what not at home means in the morning at a gentleman's door in London, so I said, very weel, as I hae had a long walk, I'll e'en rest myself and wait till he come; and with that, I plumpit down on one of the mahogany chairs in the trance.[5] The lad, seeing that I was na to be jookit,[6] upon this answered me, by saying, he would go and enquire if his master would be at home to me; and the short and the long o't was, that I got at last an audience o' my honourable friend.

' "Well, Bailie," said he, "I'm glad to see you in London," and a hantle[7] o' ither courtly glammer[8] that's no worth a repetition; and from less to mair, we proceeded to sift into the matter and end of my coming to ask the help o' his hand to get me a post in the government. But I soon saw, that wi a' the phraseology that lay at his tongue end during the election, about his power and will to serve us, his ain turn ser't, he cared little for me. Howsever, after tarrying sometime, and going to him every day, at long and last, he got me a tide-waiter's place at the

Custom-house; a poor hungry situation, no worth the grassum at a new tack of the warst land in the town's aught.[1] But minows are better than nae fish, and a tide-waiter's place was a step towards a better, if I could have waited. Luckily, however, for me, a flock of fleets and ships frae the East and West Indies came in a' thegither; and there was sic a stress for tide-waiters, that before I was sworn in and tested, I was sent down to a grand ship in the Malabar trade frae China, loaded with tea and other rich commodities; the captain whereof, a descreet man, took me down to the cabin, and gave me a dram of wine, and, when we were by oursels, he said to me,—

' "Mr. M'Lucre, what will you take to shut your eyes for an hour?"

' "I'll no take a hundred pounds," was my answer.

' "I'll make it guineas," quoth he.

'Surely, thought I, my eyne maun[2] be worth pearls and diamonds to the East India Company; so I answered and said,—

' "Captain, no to argol bargol about the matter," (for a' the time, I thought upon how I had not been sworn in;)— "what will ye gie me, if I take away my eyne out the vessel?"

' "A thousand pounds," cried he.

' "A bargain be't," said I. I think, however, had I stood out, I might hae got mair. But it does na rain thousands of pounds every day; so, to make a long tale short, I got a note of hand on the Bank of England for the sum, and, packing up my ends and my awls,[3] left the ship.

'It was my intent to have come immediately home to Scotland; but the same afternoon, I was summoned by the Board at the Custom-house for deserting my post; and the moment I went before them, they opened upon me like my lord's pack o' hounds, and said, they would send me to Newgate. "Cry, a' at ance," quoth I; "but I'll no gang." I then told them, how I was na sworn, and under no obligation to serve or obey them mair than pleasured mysel; which set them a' again a barking worse than before; whereupon, seeing no likelihood of an end to their stramash,[1] I turned mysel round, and, taking the door on my back,[2] left them, and the same night came off in the Fly[3] to Edinburgh. Since syne they have been trying every grip and wile o' the law to punish me as they threatened; but the laws of England are a great protection to the people against arbitrary power; and the letter that I have got to-day frae the Nabob, tells me, that the Commissioners hae abandoned the plea.'

Such was the account and narration that the Bailie gave to me of the particulars o' his journey to London; and when he was done, I could not but make a moral reflection or two, on the policy of gentlemen putting themselves on the leet[4] to be members of Parliament; it being a clear and plain thing, that as they are sent up to London for the benefit of the people by whom they are chosen, the people should always take care to get some of that benefit in hand paid down, otherwise they run a great risk of seeing their representatives neglecting their special interests, and treating them as entitled to no particular consideration.

CHAPTER VIII

CHOOSING A MINISTER

THE next great handling that we had in the council after the general election, was anent the choice of a minister for the parish. The Rev. Dr. Swapkirk, having had an apoplexy, the magistrates were obligated to get Mr. Pittle to be his helper. Whether it was that, by our being used to Mr. Pittle, we had ceased to have a right respect for his parts and talents, or that in reality he was but a weak brother, I cannot in conscience take it on me to say; but the certainty is, that when the Doctor departed this life, there was hardly one of the hearers who thought Mr. Pittle would ever be their placed minister, and it was as far at first from the unanimous mind of the magistrates, who are the patrons of the parish, as any thing could well be, for he was a man of no smeddum[1] in discourse. In verity, as Mrs. Pawkie my wife said, his sermons, in the warm summer afternoons, were just a perfect hushabaa, that no mortal could hearken to without sleeping. Moreover, he had a sorning[2] way with him, that the genteeler sort could na abide, for he was for ever going from house to house about tea-time, to save his ain canister. As for the young ladies, they could na endure him at all, for he had aye the sough and sound of love in his mouth, and a round-about ceremonial of joking concerning the same, that was just a fasherie[3] to them to hear. The commonality, however, were his greatest adversaries, for he was, notwithstanding the spareness of his abilities, a prideful creature, taking no interest in their hamely affairs, and seldom visiting the aged or the sick among them. Shortly, however, before the death of the Doctor, Mr. Pittle had been very attentive to my wife's full cousin, Miss Lizy Pinkie, I'll no say on account of the legacy of seven hundred pounds, left her by an uncle that made his money in foreign parts, and died at Portsmouth of the liver complaint, when he was coming home to enjoy himself; and Mrs. Pawkie told me, that as soon as Mr. Pittle could get a kirk, I need na be surprised if I heard o' a marriage between him and Miss Lizy.

Had I been a sordid and interested man, this news could never have given me the satisfaction it did, for Miss Lizy was very fond of my bairns, and it was thought that Peter would have been her heir; but so far from being concerned at what I heard, I rejoiced thereat, and resolved in secret thought, whenever a vacancy happened, Dr. Swapkirk being then fast wearing away, to exert the best of my ability to get the kirk for Mr. Pittle, not however unless he was previously married to Miss Lizy; for, to speak out, she was beginning to stand in need of a protector, and both me and Mrs. Pawkie had our fears that she might outlive her income, and in her old age become a cess[4] upon us. And it could na be said that this

was any groundless fear; for Miss Lizy, living a lonely maiden-
life by herself, with only a bit lassie to run her errands, and no
being naturally of an active or eydent[1] turn, aften wearied, and
to keep up her spirits gaed may be, now and then, oftener to the
Gardevin[2] than was just necessar, by which, as we thought,
she had a tavert[3] look. Howsever, as Mr. Pittle had taken a
notion of her, and she pleased his fancy, it was far from our
hand to misliken one that was sib[4] to us; on the contrary, it
was a duty laid on me, by the ties of blood and relationship,
to do all in my power to further their mutual affection into
matrimonial fruition; and what I did towards that end, is the
burden of this current chapter.

Dr. Swapkirk, in whom the spark of life was long fading,
closed his eyes, and it went utterly out, as to this world, on a
Saturday night, between the hours of eleven and twelve. We
had that afternoon got an inkling that he was drawing near to
his end. At the latest, Mrs. Pawkie herself went over to the
manse, and staid till she saw him die. 'It was a pleasant end,'
she said, for he was a godly, patient man, and we were both
sorely grieved, though it was a thing for which we had been
long prepared; and indeed to his family and connections,
except for the loss of the stipend, it was a very gentle dispensation, for he had been long a heavy handful, having been
for years but, as it were, a breathing lump of mortality, groosy
and oozy and doozy,[5] his faculties being shut up and locked in
by a dumb palsy.

Having had this early intimation of the Doctor's removal
to a better world, on the Sabbath morning, when I went to
join the magistrates in the council chamber, as the usage is,
to go to the laft,[6] with the town-officers carrying their halberts
before us, according to the ancient custom of all royal
boroughs, my mind was in a degree prepared to speak to them
anent the successor. Little, however, passed at that time, and
it so happened, that, by some wonder of inspiration, (there
were however folk that said it was taken out of a book of
sermons, by one Barrow an English Divine;[7]) Mr. Pittle that

forenoon preached a discourse that made an impression, in so much, that on our way back to the council chamber I said to Provost Vintner, that then was—

'Really Mr. Pittle seems, if he would exert himself, to have a nerve. I could not have thought it was in the power of his capacity to have given us such a sermon.'

The provost thought as I did, so I replied,—

'We canna, I think, do better than keep him among us. It would, indeed, Provost, no be doing justice to the young man to pass another over his head.'

I could see that the Provost was na quite sure of what I had been saying; for he replied, that it was a matter that needed consideration.

When we separated at the Council-chamber, I threw myself in the way of Bailie Weezle, and walked home with him, our talk being on the subject of the vacancy; and I rehearsed to him what had passed between me and the Provost, saying, that the Provost had made no objection to prefer Mr. Pittle, which was the truth.

Bailie Weezle was a man no overladen with worldly wisdom, and had been chosen into the Council principally on account of being easily managed. In his business, he was originally by trade a baker in Glasgow, where he made a little money, and came to settle among us with his wife, who was a native of the town, and had her relations here. Being therefore an idle man, living on his money, and of a soft and quiet nature, he was for the reason aforesaid chosen into the Council, where he always voted on the Provost's side; for in controverted questions every one is beholden to take a part, and he thought it was his duty to side with the chief magistrate.

Having convinced the Bailie that Mr. Pittle had already, as it were, a sort of infeoffment[1] in the kirk, I called in the evening on my old predecessor in the Guildry, Bailie M'Lucre, who was not a hand to be so easily dealt with; but I knew his inclinations, and therefore I resolved to go roundly to work with him. So I asked him out to take a walk, and I led him towards the Town-moor, conversing loosely about one thing and another, and touching softly here and there on the vacancy.

When we were well on into the middle of the moor, I stopped, and, looking round me, said, 'Bailie, surely it's a great neglec of the magistrates and council to let this braw¹ broad piece of land so near the town, lie in a state o' nature, and giving pasturage to only twa-three of the poor folk's cows. I wonder you, that's now a rich man, and with eyne worth pearls and diamonds, that ye dinna think of asking a tack of this land; ye might make a great thing o't.'

The fish nibbled, and told me that he had for some time entertained a thought on the subject; but he was afraid that I would be overly extortionate.

'I wonder to hear you, Bailie,' said I; 'I trust and hope no one will ever find me out of the way of justice; and to convince you that I can do a friendly turn, I'll no objec to gie you a' my influence free gratis, if ye'll gie Mr. Pittle a lift into the kirk; for, to be plain with you, the worthy young man, who, as ye heard to-day, is no without an ability, has long been fond of Mrs. Pawkie's cousin, Miss Lizy Pinkie; and I would fain do all that lies in my power to help on the match.

The bailie was well pleased with my frankness, and before returning home we came to a satisfactory understanding; so that the next thing I had to do, was to see Mr. Pittle himself on the subject. Accordingly, in the gloaming, I went over to where he staid: it was with Miss Jenny Killfuddy, an elderly maiden lady whose father was the minister of Braehill, and the same that is spoken of in the Chronicle of Dalmailing,² as having had his eye almost put out by a clash of glar,³ at the stormy placing of Mr. Balwhidder.

'Mr. Pittle,' said I, as soon as I was in and the door closed. 'I'm come to you as a friend; both Mrs. Pawkie and me have long discerned that ye have had a look more than common towards our friend,⁴ Miss Lizy, and we think it our duty to inquire your intents, before matters gang to greater length.'

He looked a little dumb-foundered at this salutation, and was at a loss for an answer, so I continued—

'If your designs be honourable, and no doubt they are, now's your time; strike while the iron's hot. By the death of the Doctor, the kirk's vacant, the town council have the patronage; and if ye marry Miss Lizy, my interest and influence shall not be slack in helping you into the poopit.' In short, out of what passed that night, on the Monday following Mr. Pittle and Miss Lizy were married, and by my dexterity, together with the able help I had in Bailie M'Lucre, he was in due season placed and settled in the parish; and the next year more than fifty acres of the Town-moor were inclosed, on a nine hundred and ninety-nine years' tack, at an easy rate between me and the Bailie, he paying the half of the expence of the ditching and rooting out of the whins[1]; and it was acknowledged by every one that saw it, that there had not been a greater improvement for many years in all the country side. But to the best actions, there will be adverse and discontented spirits; and, on this occasion, there were not wanting persons naturally of a disloyal opposition temper, who complained of the inclosure as a usurpation of the rights and property of the poorer burghers. Such revilings, however, are what all persons in authority must suffer; and they had only the effect of making me button my coat, and look out the crooser[2] to the blast.

CHAPTER IX

AN EXECUTION

THE attainment of honours and dignities is not enjoyed without a portion of trouble and care, which, like a shadow, follows all temporalities. On the very evening of the same day that I was first chosen to be a bailie,[3] a sore affair came to light, in the discovery that Jean Gaisling had murdered her bastard bairn. She was the daughter of a donsie[1] mother that could gie no name to her gets,[2] of which she had two laddies, besides Jean; the one of them had gone off with the soldiers some time before, the other, a douce well-behaved callan,[3] was in my lord's servitude, as a stable-boy at the castle. Jeanie herself was the bonniest lassie in the whole town, but light-headed, and fonder of outgait and blether in the causey[4] than was discreet of one of her uncertain parentage. She was at the time when she met with her misfortune in the service of Mrs. Dalrymple, a colonel's widow, that came out of the army, and settled among us on her jointure.

This Mrs. Dalrymple, having been long used to the loose morals of camps and regiments, did not keep that strict hand over poor Jeanie, and her other serving lass, that she ought to have done, and so the poor guideless creature fell into the snare of some of the neer-doe-weel gentlemen that used to play cards at night with Mrs. Dalrymple. The truths of the story were never well known, nor who was the father, for the tragical issue barred all enquiry; but it came out that poor Jeanie was left to herself, and being instigated by the Enemy, after she had been delivered, did, while the midwife's back was turned, strangle the baby with a napkin. She was discovered in the very fact with the bairn black in the face in the bed beside her.

The heinousness of the crime can by no possibility be lessened; but the beauty of the mother, her tender years, and her light-headedness, had won many favourers, and there was a great leaning in the hearts of all the town to compassionate her, especially when they thought of the ill example that had been set to her in the walk and conversation of her mother. It was not, however, within the power of the magistrates to overlook the accusation; so we were obligated to cause a precognition[5] to be taken, and the search left no doubt of the wilfulness of the murder. Jeanie was in consequence removed to the Tolbooth,[6] where she lay till the lords[7] were coming to Ayr, when she was sent thither to stand her trial before them; but, from the hour she did the deed, she never spoke.

Her trial was a short procedure, and she was cast to be hanged—and not only to be hanged, but ordered to be executed in our town, and her body given to the doctors to make an Atomy. The execution of Jeanie was what all expected would happen; but when the news reached the town of the other parts of the sentence, the wail was as the sough of a pestilence, and fain would the council have got it dispensed with. But the Lord Advocate[1] was just wud[2] at the crime, both because there had been no previous concealment, so as to have been an extenuation for the shame of the birth, and because Jeanie would neither divulge the name of the father, nor make answer to all the interrogatories that were put to her, standing at the bar like a dumbie, and looking round her, and at the judges, like a demented creature, and beautiful as a Flanders' baby.[3] It was thought by many, that her advocate might have made great use of her visible consternation, and pled that she was by herself;[4] for in truth she had every appearance of being so. He was, however, a dure man, no doubt well enough versed in the particulars and punctualities of the law for an ordinary plea, but no of the right sort of knowledge and talent to take up the case of a forlorn lassie, misled by ill example and a winsome nature, and clothed in the allurement of loveliness, as the judge himself said to the jury.

On the night before the day of execution, she was brought over in a chaise from Ayr between two town-officers, and placed again in our hands, and still she never spoke.

Nothing could exceed the compassion that every one had for poor Jeanie, so she was na committed to a common cell, but laid in the council room, where the ladies of the town made up a comfortable bed for her, and some of them sat up all night and prayed for her; but her thoughts were gone, and she sat silent.

In the morning, by break of day, her wanton mother that had been trolloping in Glasgow came to the Tolbooth door, and made a dreadful wally waeing, and the ladies were obligated, for the sake of peace, to bid her be let in. But Jeanie noticed her not, still sitting with her eyes cast down, waiting the coming on of the hour of her doom. The wicked mother first tried to rouse her by weeping and distraction, and then she took to upbraiding; but Jeanie seemed to heed her not, save only once, and then she but looked at the misleart tinkler,[1] and shook her head. I happened to come into the room at this time, and seeing all the charitable ladies weeping around, and the randy mother talking to the poor lassie as loudly and vehement as if she had been both deaf and sullen, I commanded the officers, with a voice of authority, to remove the mother, by which we had for a season peace, till the hour came.

There had not been an execution in the town in the memory of the oldest person then living; the last that suffered was one of the martyrs in the time of the persecution,[2] so that we were not skilled in the business, and had besides no hangman, but were necessitated to borrow the Ayr one. Indeed, I being the youngest bailie, was in terror that the obligation might have fallen on me.

A scaffold was erected at the Tron[3] just under the Tolbooth windows, by Thomas Gimblet, the Master-of-work, who had a good penny of profit by the job, for he contracted with the town council, and had the boards after the business was done to the bargain; but Thomas was then deacon of the wrights, and himself a member of our body.[4]

At the hour appointed, Jeanie, dressed in white, was led out by the town-officers, and in the midst of the magistrates from among the ladies, with her hands tied behind her with a black ribbon. At the first sight of her at the Tolbooth stairhead, a universal sob rose from all the multitude, and the sternest ee[5] could na refrain from shedding a tear. We marched slowly down the stair, and on to the foot of the scaffold, where her younger brother, Willy, that was stable-boy at my lord's, was standing by himself, in an open ring made round him in the crowd; every one compassionating the dejected laddie, for he was a fine youth, and of an orderly spirit.

As his sister came towards the foot of the ladder, he ran

towards her, and embraced her with a wail of sorrow that melted every heart, and made us all stop in the middle of our solemnity. Jeanie looked at him, (for her hands were tied,) and a silent tear was seen to drop from her cheek. But in the course of little more than a minute, all was quiet, and we[1] proceeded to ascend the scaffold. Willy, who had by this time dried his eyes, went up with us, and when Mr. Pittle had said the prayer, and sung the psalm, in which the whole multitude joined, as it were with the contrition of sorrow, the hangman stepped forward to put on the fatal cap, but Willy took it out of his hand, and placed it on his sister himself, and then kneeling down, with his back towards her, closing his eyes and shutting his ears with his hands, he saw not, nor heard when she was launched into eternity.

When the awful act was over, and the stir was for the magistrates to return, and the body to be cut down, poor Willy rose, and, without looking round, went down the steps of the scaffold; the multitude made a lane for him to pass, and he went on through them hiding his face, and gaed straight out of the town. As for the mother, we were obligated, in the course of the same year, to drum her out of the town, for stealing thirteen choppin[2] bottles from William Gallon's, the vintner's, and selling them for whiskey to Maggy Picken, that was tried at the same time for the reset.[3]

CHAPTER X

A RIOT

NOTHING very material, after Jeanie Gaisling's affair, happened in the town, till the time of my first provostry, when an event arose with an aspect of exceeding danger to the lives and properties of the whole town. I cannot indeed think of it at this day, though age has cooled me down in all concerns to a spirit of composure, without feeling the blood boil in my veins, so greatly, in the matter alluded to, was the King's dignity and the rightful government by law and magistracy, insulted in my person.

From time out of mind, it had been an ancient and commendable custom in the borough, to have, on the King's birthday, a large bowl of punch made in the council chamber, in order and to the end and effect of drinking his Majesty's health at the cross; and for pleasance to the commonality, the magistrates were wont, on the same occasion, to allow a cart of coals for a bonfire.[1] I do not now, at this distance of time, remember the cause how it came to pass, but come to pass it did, that the council resolved for time coming to refrain from giving the coals for the bonfire; and it so fell out, that the first administration of this economy was carried into effect during my provostry, and the wyte[2] of it was laid at my door by the trades lads, and others, that took on them the lead in hobbleshows at the fairs, and such like public doings. Now I come to the issue and particulars.

The birth-day, in progress of time, came round, and the morning was ushered in with the ringing of bells, and the windows of the houses adorned with green boughs and garlands. It was a fine bright day, and nothing could exceed the glee and joviality of all faces till the afternoon, when I went up to the council-chamber in the Tolbooth, to meet the other magistrates and respectable characters of the town, in order to drink the King's health. In going thither, I was joined, just as I was stepping out of my shop, by Mr. Stoup, the Excise gauger, and Mr. Firlot, the meal-monger, who had made a power of money a short time before, by a cargo of corn that he had brought from Belfast, the ports being then open, for which he was envied by some, and by the common sort was considered and reviled as a wicked hard-hearted forestaller. As for Mr. Stoup, although he was a very creditable man, he had the repute of being overly austere in his vocation, for which he was not liked, over and above the dislike that the commonality cherish against all of his calling, so that it was not possible that any magistrate, such as I endeavoured to be, adverse to ill-doers, and to vice and immorality of every kind, could have met at such a time and juncture, a greater misfortune than those two men, especially when it is considered, that the abolition of the bonfire was regarded as a heinous trespass on the liberties and privileges of the people. However, having left the shop, and being joined, as I have narrated, by Mr. Stoup and Mr. Firlot, we walked together at a sedate pace towards the Tolbooth, before which, and at the cross, a great assemblage of people were convened; trades lads, weavers with coats out at the elbow, the callans of the school; in short, the utmost gathering and congregation of the clanjamphry,[1] who, the moment they saw me coming, set up a great shout and howl, crying like disperation, 'Provost, whar's the bonfire? Hae ye sent the coals, Provost, hame to yoursel, or selt them, Provost, for meal to the forestaller?' with other such misleart[2] phraseology that was most contemptuous, bearing every symptom of the rebellion and insurrection that they were then meditating. But I kept my temper, and went into the council-chamber, where others of the respectable inhabitants were met with the magistrates and town-council assembled.

'What's the matter, Provost?' said several of them as I came in; 'are ye ill, or what has fashed[3] you?' But I only replied, that the mob without was very unruly for being deprived of their bonfire. Upon this, some of those present proposed to gratify them, by ordering a cart of coals, as usual; but I set my face against this, saying, that it would look like intimidation were we now to comply, and that all veneration for law and authority would be at an end by such weakness on the part of those entrusted with the exercise of power. There the debate, for a season, ended; and the punch being ready, the table was taken out of the council-chamber, and carried to the cross, and placed there, and then the bowl and glasses; the magistrates following, and the rest of the company.

Seeing us surrounded by the town-officers with their

halberts,[1] the multitude made way seemingly with their wonted civility, and when His Majesty's health[2] was drank, they shouted with us, seemingly too as loyally as ever; but that was a traitorous device to throw us off our guard, as, in the upshot, was manifested; for no sooner had we filled the glasses again, than some of the most audacious of the rioters began to insult us, crying, 'The bonfire! the bonfire!—No fire, no bowl!—Gentle and semple should share and share alike.' In short, there was a moving backwards and forwards, and a confusion among the mob, with snatches of huzzas and laughter, that boded great mischief, and some of my friends near me said to me no to be alarmed, which only alarmed me the more, as I thought they surely had heard something. However, we drank our second glass without any actual molestation, but when we gave the three cheers, as the custom was, after the same, instead of being answered joyfully, the mob set up a frightful yell, and rolling like the waves of the sea, came on us with such a shock, that the table, and punch-bowl, and glasses, were couped[3] and broken. Bailie Weezle, who was standing on the opposite side, got his shins so ruffled by the falling of the table, that he was for many a day after confined to the house with two sore legs, and it was feared he would have been a lameter for life.

The dinging down of the table was the signal of the rebellious ringleaders for open war. Immediately there was an outcry and a roaring, that was a terrification to hear; and I know not how it was, but before we kent where we were, I found myself, with many of those who had been drinking the King's health, once more in the council-chamber, where it was proposed that we should read the riot act from the windows, and this awful duty, by the nature of my office as Provost, it behoved me to perform. Nor did I shrink from it; for by this time my corruption was raised, and I was determined not to let the royal authority be set at nought in my hands.

Accordingly, Mr. Keelivine,[4] the town-clerk, having searched out among his law books for the riot act, one of the windows of the council-chamber was opened, and the bellman having, with a loud voice, proclaimed the 'O yes,' three times; I stepped forward with the book in my hands. At the sight of me, the rioters, in the most audacious manner, set up a blasphemous laugh; but instead of finding me daunted thereat, they were surprised at my fortitude, and when I began to read they listened in silence. But this was a concerted stratagem; for the moment that I had ended, a dead cat came whizzing through the air like a comet, and gave me such a clash in the face, that I was knocked down to the floor, in the middle of the very council-chamber. What ensued is neither to be told nor described; some were for beating the fire-drum,[1] others were for arming ourselves with what weapons were in the Tolbooth; but I deemed it more congenial to the nature of the catastrophe, to send off an express to Ayr, for the regiment of soldiers that was quartered there:—the roar of the rioters without being all the time like a raging flood.

Major Targot, however, who had seen service in foreign wars, was among us, and he having tried in vain to get us to listen to him, went out of his own accord to the rioters, and was received by them with three cheers. He then spoke to them in an exhorting manner, and represented to them the imprudence of their behaviour; upon which they gave him three other cheers, and immediately dispersed and went home. The Major was a vain bodie, and took great credit to himself, as I heard, for this; but, considering the temper of mind the mob was at one time in, it is quite evident that it was no so much the Major's speech and exhortation that sent them off, as their dread and terror of the soldiers, that I had sent for.

All that night the magistrates, with other gentlemen of the town, sat in the council-chamber, and sent out, from time to time, to see that every thing was quiet; and by this judicious proceeding, of which we drew up and transmitted a full account to the King and government, in London, by whom the whole of our conduct was highly applauded, peace was maintained till the next day at noon, when a detachment, as it was called,[1] of four companies came from the regiment in Ayr, and took upon them the preservation of order and regularity. I may here notice, that this was the first time any soldiers had been quartered in the town, since the forty-five;[2] and a woeful warning it was of the consequences that follow rebellion and treasonable practices, for, to the present day, we have always had a portion of every regiment, sent to Ayr, quartered upon us.

CHAPTER XI

POLICY

ABOUT the end of my first provostry, I began to make a discovery. Whether it was that I was a little inordinately lifted up by reason of the dignity, and did not comport myself with a sufficient condescension and conciliation of manner to the rest of the town-council, it would be hard to say. I could, however, discern that a general ceremonious insincerity was performed by the members towards me, especially on the part of those who were in league and conjunct with the town-clerk, who comported himself, by reason of his knowledge of the law, as if he was in verity the true and effectual chief magistrate of the borough; and the effect of this discovery, was a consideration and digesting within me how I should demean myself, so as to regain the vantage I had lost; taking little heed as to how the loss had come, whether from an ill-judged pride and pretending in myself, or from the natural spirit of envy, that darkens the good will of all mankind towards those who get sudden promotion, as it was commonly thought I had obtained, in being so soon exalted to the provostry.

Before the Michaelmas, I was, in consequence of this deliberation and councelling with my own mind, fully prepared to achieve a great stroke of policy for the future govern-

ment of the town. I saw that it would not do for me for a time
to stand overly eminent forward, and that it was a better
thing, in the world, to have power and influence, than to show
the possession of either. Accordingly, after casting about from
one thing to another, I bethought with myself, that it would
be a great advantage if the council could be worked with, so as
to nominate and appoint My Lord the next provost[1] after me.
In the proposing of this, I could see there would be no difficulty; but the hazard was, that his lordship might only be
made a tool of instrumentality to our shrewd and sly town-
clerk, Mr. Keelivine, while it was of great importance, that I
should keep the management of My Lord in my own hands.
In this straight, however, a thing came to pass, which strongly
confirms me in the opinion, that good luck, has really a great
deal to say with the prosperity of men. The Earl, who had not
for years been in the country, came down in the summer from
London, and I, together with the other magistrates and
council, received an invitation to dine with him at the castle.
We all of course went, 'with our best breeding,' as the old
proverb says, 'helped by our brawest cleeding[2];' but I soon
saw, that it was only a *pro forma* dinner, and that there was
nothing of cordiality in all the civility with which we were
treated, both by my lord and my lady. Nor, indeed, could I,
on an after-thought, blame our noble entertainers for being
so on their guard; for in truth some of the deacons,[3] (I'll no
say any of the bailies,) were so transported out of themselves
with the glory of my lord's banquet, and the thought of dining
at the castle, and at the first table too, that when the wine
began to fiz in their noddles, they forgot themselves entirely,
and made no more of the Earl than if he had been one of themselves. Seeing to what issue the matter was tending, I set a
guard upon myself; and while my lord, out of a parly-voo
politess, was egging them on, one after another, to drink
deeper and deeper of his old wines, to the manifest detriment
of their own senses, I kept myself in a degree as sober as a
judge, warily noting all things that came to pass.

The Earl had really a commendable share of common sense for a lord; and the discretion of my conduct was not unnoticed by him; in so much, that after the major part of the council had become, as it may be said, out o' the bodie,[1] cracking their jokes with one another, just as if all present had been carousing at the Cross-Keys, his lordship wised[2] to me to come and sit beside him, where we had a very private and satisfactory conversation together; in the which conversation, I said, that it was a pity he would not allow himself to be nominated our Provost. Nobody had ever minted[3] to him a thought of the thing before, so it was no wonder that his lordship replied, with a look of surprise, saying, 'that so far from refusing, he had never heard of any such proposal.'

'That is very extraordinary, my lord,' said I, 'for surely it is for your interests, and would to a certainty be a great advantage to the town, were your lordship to take upon you the nominal office of provost; I say nominal, my lord, because being now used to the duties, and somewhat experienced therein, I could take all the necessary part of the trouble off your lordship's hands, and so render the provostry in your lordship's name a perfect nonentity.' Whereupon, he was pleased to say, if I would do so, and he commended my talents and prudence, he would have no objection to be made the provost at the ensuing election. Something more explicit might have ensued at that time, but Bailie M'Lucre and Mr. Sharpset, who was the Dean of Guild, had been for about the space of half an hour carrying on a vehement argument anent some concern of the guildry, in which, coming to high words, and both being beguiled and ripened into folly by the Earl's wine, they came into such a manifest quarrel, that Mr. Sharpset pulled off the Bailie's best wig, and flung it with a damn into the fire: the which stramash[4] caused my lord to end the sederunt[5]; but none of the magistrates, save myself, was in a condition to go with his lordship to My Lady in the drawing-room.

CHAPTER XII

THE SPY

SHORTLY after the foregoing transaction, a thing happened, that, in a manner, I would fain conceal and suppress from the knowledge of future times, although it was but a sort of sprose[1] to make the world laugh. Fortunately for my character, however, it did not fall out exactly in my hands, although it happened in the course of my provostry. The matter spoken of, was the affair of a Frenchman, who was taken up as a spy; for the American war was then raging, and the French[2] had taken the part of the Yankie rebels.

One day, in the month of August it was, I had gone on some private concernment of my own to Kilmarnock, and Mr. Booble, who was then oldest bailie, naturally officiated as chief magistrate in my stead.

There had been, as the world knows, a disposition on the part of the Grand Monarque[3] of that time, to invade and conquer this country, the which made it a duty incumbent on all magistrates to keep a vigilant eye on the in-comings and out-goings of aliens and other suspectable persons. On the said day, and during my absence, a Frenchman, that could speak no manner of English, somehow was discovered in the Cross-Key inns. What he was, or where he came from, nobody at the time could tell, as I was informed; but there he was, having come into the house, at the door, with a bundle in his hand, and a portmanty on his shoulder, like a traveller out of some vehicle of conveyance. Mrs. Drammer, the landlady, did not like his looks, for he had toozy[4] black whiskers, was lank and wan, and moreover deformed beyond human nature, as she said, with a parrot nose, and had no cravat, but only a bit black ribbon drawn through two button-holes, fastening his ill-coloured sark neck,[5] which gave him altogether something of an unwholesome, outlandish appearance.

Finding he was a foreigner, and understanding that strict injunctions were laid on the magistrates by the King and Government anent the egressing of such persons, she thought, for the credit of her house, and the safety of the community at large, that it behoved her to send word to me, then Provost, of this man's visibility among us; but as I was not at home, Mrs. Pawkie, my wife, directed the messenger to Bailie Booble's. The Bailie was, at all times, overly ready to claught¹ at an alarm; and when he heard the news, he went straight to the council-room, and sending for the rest of the council, ordered the alien enemy, as he called the forlorn Frenchman, to be brought before him. By this time, the suspicion of a spy in the town had spread far and wide; and Mrs. Pawkie told me, that there was a palid consternation in every countenance when the black and yellow man, for he had not the looks of the honest folks of this country, was brought up the street between two of the town-officers, to stand an examine before Bailie Booble.

Neither the Bailie, nor those that were then sitting with him, could speak any French language, and 'the alien enemy' was as little master of our tongue. I have often wondered, how the Bailie did not jealouse² that he could be no spy, seeing how, in that respect, he wanted the main faculty. But he was under the enchantment of a panic, partly thinking, also, perhaps, that he was to do a great exploit for the government in my absence.

However, the man was brought before him, and there was he, and them all, speaking loud out to one another as if they had been hard of hearing, when I, on my coming home from Kilmarnock, went to see what was going on in the council. Considering that the procedure had been in hand some time before my arrival, I thought it judicious to leave the whole business with those present, and to sit still as a spectator; and really it was very comical to observe how the Bailie was driven to his wits-end by the poor lean and yellow Frenchman; and in what a pucker of passion the pannel³ put himself at every new interlocutor, none of which he could understand. At last, the Bailie getting no satisfaction,—how could he? he directed the man's portmanty and bundle to be opened; and in the bottom of the fore-mentioned package, there, to be sure, was found many a mystical and suspicious paper which no one could read; among others, there was a strange map, as it then seemed to all present.

'I' gude faith,' cried the Bailie, with a keckle of exultation, 'here's proof enough now. This is a plain map o' the Frith o' Clyde, all the way to the tail of the bank o' Greenock. This muckle place is Arran; that round ane is the craig of Ailsa; the wee ane between is Plada. Gentlemen, gentlemen, this is a sore discovery; there will be hanging and quartering on this.' So he ordered the man to be forthwith committed as a king's prisoner to the Tolbooth; and turning to me, said:— 'My Lord Provost, as ye have not been present throughout the whole of this troublesome affair, I'll e'en gie an account mysel to the Lord Advocate of what we have done.' I thought, at the time, there was something fey[1] and overly forward in this, but I assented; for I know not what it was, that seemed to me as if there was something neither right nor regular; indeed, to say the truth, I was no ill pleased, that the Bailie took on him what he did; so I allowed him to write himself to the Lord Advocate; and, as the sequel shewed, it was a blessed prudence on my part that I did so. For no sooner did his lordship receive the Bailie's terrifying letter, than a special king's messenger was sent to take the spy into Edinburgh Castle; and nothing could surpass the great importance that Bailie Booble made of himself, on the occasion, of getting the man into a coach, and two dragoons to guard him into Glasgow.

But, O, what a dejected man was the miserable Bailie Booble, and what a laugh rose from shop and chamber, when the tidings came out from Edinburgh, that 'the alien enemy' was but a French cook coming over from Dublin, with the intent to take up the trade of a confectioner in Glasgow; and that the map of the Clyde was nothing but a plan for the outset of a fashionable table. The Bailie's island of Arran being the

roast beef, and the craig of Ailsa the plumb-pudding, and
Plada a butter-boat. Nobody enjoyed the jocularity of the
business more than myself; but I trembled, when I thought
of the escape that my honour and character had with the
Lord Advocate. I trow, Bailie Booble never set himself so
forward from that day to this.

CHAPTER XIII

THE MEAL MOB

AFTER the close of the American war,[1] I had, for various
reasons of a private nature, a wish to sequestrate myself for a
time, from any very ostensible part in public affairs. Still,
however, desiring to retain a mean of resuming my station,
and of maintaining my influence in the council, I bespoke Mr.
Keg to act in my place as deputy for My Lord, who was regularly every year at this time chosen into the provostry.

This Mr. Keg was a man who had made a competency by
the Isle-of-Man trade, and had come in from the Laighlands,
where he had been apparently in the farming line, to live
among us; but for many a day, on account of something that
happened when he was concerned in the smuggling, he kept
himself cannily aloof from all sort of town matters, deporting
himself with a most creditable sobriety; in so much, that there
was at one time a sough that Mr. Pittle, the minister, our friend,
had put him on the leet[2] for an elder. That post, however, if it
was offered to him, he certainly never accepted; but I jealouse
that he took the rumour o't for a sign that his character had
ripened into an estimation among us, for he thenceforth began
to kithe[3] more in public, and was just a patron to every mani-
festation of loyalty, putting more lights in his windows in the
rejoicing nights of victory than any other body, Mr. M'Creesh,
the candlemaker, and Collector Cocket, not excepted. Thus,

in the fulness of time, he was taken into the council, and no man in the whole corporation could be said to be more zealous than he was. In respect, therefore, to him, I had nothing to fear, so far as the interests and, over and above all, the loyalty of the corporation were concerned; but something like a quailing came over my heart, when, after the breaking up of the council on the day of election, he seemed to shy away from me, who had been instrumental to his advancement. However, I trow he had soon reason to repent of that ingratitude, as I may well call it, for when the troubles of the meal mob came upon him, I showed him that I could keep my distance as well as my neighbours.

It was on the Friday our market-day,[1] that the hobble-shaw[2] began, and in the afternoon, when the farmers who had brought in their victual for sale were loading their carts to take it home again, the price not having come up to their expectation. All the forenoon, as the wives that went to the meal-market, came back railing with toom pocks and basins, it might have been foretold, that the farmers would have to abate their extortion, or that something would come o't before night. My new house and shop being forenent[3] the market, I had noted this, and said to Mrs. Pawkie, my wife, what I thought would be the upshot, especially when, towards the afternoon, I observed the commonality gathering in the market-place, and no sparing in their tongues to the farmers; so, upon her advice, I directed Thomas Snakers to put on the shutters.

Some of the farmers were loading their carts to go home, when the schools skailed,[4] and all the weans came shouting to the market. Still nothing happened, till tinkler Jean, a randy[5] that had been with the army at the siege of Gibraltar, and, for aught I ken, in the Americas, if no in the Indies likewise;— she came with her meal-basin in her hand, swearing like a trooper, that if she did na get it filled with meal at fifteen-pence a peck,[6] (the farmers demanded sixteen,) she would have the fu o't of their hearts' blood; and the mob of thoughtless weans and idle fellows, with shouts and yells, encouraged Jean, and egged her on to a catastrophe. The corruption[1] of the farmers was thus raised, and a young rash lad, the son of James Dyke o' the Mount, whom Jean was blackguarding at a dreadful rate, and upbraiding on account of some ploy he had had with the Dalmailing Session anent a bairn,[2] in an unguarded moment lifted his hand, and shook his neive[3] in Jean's face, and even, as she said, struck her. He himself swore an affidavit that he gave her only a ding out of his way; but be this as it may, at him rushed Jean, with open mouth, and broke her timber meal-basin on his head, as it had been an egg shell. Heaven only knows what next ensued; but in a jiffy the whole market-place was as white with scattered meal as if it had been covered with snow, and the farmers were seen flying helter skelter out at the townhead, pursued by the mob, in a hail and whirlwind of stones and glar. Then the drums were heard beating to arms, and the soldiers were seen flying to their rendezvous. I stood composedly at the dining-room window, and was very thankful that I was na Provost in such a hurricane, when I saw poor Mr. Keg, as pale as a dish-clout, running to and fro bareheaded, with the town-officers and their halberts at his heels, exhorting and crying, till he was as hoarse as a crow, to the angry multitude that was raging and tossing like a sea in the market-place. Then it was that he felt the consequence of his pridefulness towards me; for, observing me standing in serenity at the window, he came, and in a vehement manner cried to me for the love of Heaven to come to his assistance, and pacify the people. It would not have been proper in me to have refused; so out I went in the very nick of time, for when I got to the door, there was the soldiers in battle array, coming marching with fife and drum up the gait[4] with Major Blaze at their head, red and furious in the face, and bent on some bloody business. The first thing I did was to run to the Major, just as he was facing the men for a 'charge bagonets' on the people, crying to him to halt, for the riot act was na yet read, and the murder of all that might be slain would lie at his door; at which to hear he stood aghast, and the men halted. Then I flew back to the Provost, and I cried to him, 'Read the riot act!' which some of the mob hearing, became terrified thereat, none knowing the penalties or consequences thereof, when backed by soldiers; and in a moment, as if they had seen the glimpse of a terrible spirit in the air, the whole multitude dropped the dirt and stones out of their hands, and turning their backs, flew into doors and closes[1], and were skailed[2] before we knew where we were. It is not to be told the laud and admiration that I got for my ability in this business; for the Major was so well pleased to have been saved from a battle, that, at my suggestion, he wrote an account of the whole business to the commander-in-chief, assuring him that, but for me, and my great weight and authority in the town, nobody could tell what the issue might have been; so that the Lord Advocate,[3] to whom the report was shown by the general, wrote me a letter of thanks in the name of the government; and I, although not Provost, was thus seen and believed to be a person of the foremost note and consideration in the town.

But although the mob was dispersed, as I have related, the consequences did not end there; for, the week following, none of the farmers brought in their victual; and there was a great lamentation and moaning in the market-place, when, on the Friday, not a single cart from the country was to be seen, but only Simon Laidlaw's, with his timber capps and luggies;[4] and the talk was, that meal would be half-a-crown the peck. The grief, however, of the business was na visible till the Saturday, the wonted day for the poor to seek their meat, when the swarm of beggars that came forth was a sight truly calamitous. Many a decent auld woman that had patiently eked out the slender thread of a weary life with her wheel, in privacy, her scant and want known only to her Maker, was seen going from door to door, with the salt tear in her e'e, and looking in the face of the pitiful, being as yet unacquainted with the language of beggary; but the worst sight of all, was two bonny bairns, drest in their best, of a genteel demeanour, going from house to house, like the hungry babes in the wood; nobody kent who they were, nor whar they came from; but as I was seeing them served myself at our door, I spoke to them, and they told me, that their mother was lying sick and ill at home. They were the orphans of a broken merchant from Glasgow, and, with their mother, had come out to our town the week before, without knowing where else to seek their meat.

Mrs. Pawkie, who was a tender-hearted mother herself, took in the bairns on hearing this, and we made of them, and the same night, among our acquaintance, we got a small sum raised to assist their mother, who proved a very well bred and respectable lady-like creature. When she got better, she was persuaded to take up a school, which she kept for some years, with credit to herself and benefit to the community, till she got a legacy left her by a brother that died in India, the which, being some thousands, caused her to remove into Edinburgh, for the better education of her own children, and it's seldom that legacies are so well bestowed, for she never forgot Mrs. Pawkie's kindness, and out of the fore-end of her wealth she sent her a very handsome present. Divers matters of elegance have come to us from her, year by year, since syne,[1] and regularly on the anniversary-day of that sore Saturday, as the Saturday following the meal mob[2] was ever after called.

CHAPTER XIV

THE SECOND PROVOSTRY

I HAVE had occasion to observe in the course of my experience, that there is not a greater mollifier of the temper and nature of man than a constant flowing in of success and prosperity. From the time that I had been Dean of Guild, I was sensible of a considerable increase of my worldly means and substance; and although Bailie M'Lucre played me a soople trick at the election, by the inordinate sale and roup of his potatoe-rig, the which tried me, as I do confess, and nettled me with disappointment; yet things, in other respects, went so well with me, that about the eighty-eight,[1] I began to put forth my hand again into public affairs, endowed both with more vigour and activity than it was in the first period of my magisterial functions. Indeed, it may be here proper for me to narrate, that my retiring into the back-ground, during the last two or three years, was a thing, as I have said, done on mature deliberation; partly, in order that the weight of my talents might be rightly estimated; and, partly, that men might, of their own reflections, come to a proper understanding concerning them. I did not secede from the council. Could I have done that with propriety, I would assuredly not have scrupled to make the sacrifice; but I knew well, that, if I was to resign, it would not be easy afterwards to get myself again chosen in. In a word, I was persuaded that I had, at times, carried things a little too highly, and that I had the adversary of a rebellious feeling in the minds and hearts of the corporation against me. However, what I did, answered the end and purpose I had in view; folk began to wonder and think with themselves, what for Mr. Pawkie had ceased to bestir himself in public affairs; and the magistrates and council, having on two or three occasions done very unsatisfactory things, it was said by one, and echoed by another, till the whole town was persuaded of the fact, that, had I lent my shoulder to the wheel, things would not have been as they were. But the matter which did the most service to me at this time, was a rank piece of idolatry towards My Lord, on the part of Bailie M'Lucre, who had again got himself most sickerly[2] installed in the Guildry. Sundry tacks came to an end in this year of eighty-eight; and, among others, the Niggerbrae-park, which, lying at a commodious distance from the town, might have been re-let with a rise and advantage. But what did the Dean of Guild do?

He, in some secret and clandestine manner, gave a hint to My Lord's factor, to make an offer for the park on a two nineteen years' lease, at the rent then going; the which was done in My Lord's name, his lordship being then Provost. The Nigger-brae was accordingly let to him, at the same rent which the town received for it in the sixty-nine. Nothing could be more manifest than that there was some jookerie cookerie[1] in this affair; but in what manner it was done, or how the Dean of Guild's benefit was to ensue, no one could tell, and few were able to conjecture; for My Lord was sorely straitened for money, and had nothing to spare out of hand. However, towards the end of the year, a light broke in upon us.

Gabriel M'Lucre, the Dean of Guild's fifth son, a fine spirited laddie, somehow got suddenly a cadetcy to go to India; and there were uncharitably-minded persons, who said, that this was the payment for the Niggerbrae job to My Lord. The outcry,[2] in consequence, both against the Dean of Guild, and especially against the magistrates and council for consenting thereto, was so extraordinary, and I was so openly upbraided for being so long lukewarm, that I was, in a manner, forced again forward to take a prominent part; but I took good care to let it be well known, that, in resuming my public faculties, I was resolved to take my own way, and to introduce a new method and reformation into all our concerns. Accordingly, at the Michaelmas following, that is, in the eighty-nine, I was a second time chosen to the Provostry; with an understanding, that I was to be upheld in the office and dignity for two years; and that sundry improvements, which I thought the town was susceptible of, both in the causey of the streets and the reparation of the kirk, should be set about under my direction; but the way in which I handled the same, and brought them to a satisfactory com-pleteness and perfection, will supply abundant matter for two chapters.

CHAPTER XV

THE IMPROVEMENT OF THE STREETS

IN ancient times, Gudetown had been fortified with ports and gates at the end of the streets; and in troublesome occasions, the country people, as the traditions relate, were in the practice of driving in their families and cattle for shelter. This gave occasion to that great width in our streets, and those of other royal boroughs, which is so remarkable; the same being so built, to give room and stance for the cattle. But in those days, the streets were not paved at the sides, but only in the middle, or, as it was called, the crown of the causey; which was raised and backed upward, to let the rain-water run off into the gutters. In progress of time, however, as the land and kingdom gradually settled down into an orderly state, the farmers and country folk having no cause to drive in their herds and flocks, as in the primitive ages of a rampageous antiquity, the proprietors of houses in the town, at their own cost, began, one after another, to pave the spaces of ground between their steadings[1] and the crown of the causey; the which spaces were called lones,[2] and the lones being considered as private property, the corporation had only regard to the middle portion of the street; that which I have said was named the crown of the causey.

The effect of this separation of interests in a common good began to manifest itself, when the pavement[3] of the crown of the causey, by neglect, became rough and dangerous to loaded carts and gentlemen's carriages passing through the town; in so much, that, for some time prior to my second Provostry, the carts and carriages made no hesitation of going over the lones, instead of keeping the highway in the middle of the street; at which, many of the burgesses made loud and just complaints.

One dark night, the very first Sunday after my restoration to the Provostry, there was like to have happened a very sore thing by an old woman, one Peggy Waife, who had been out with her gowntail over her head for a choppin[1] of strong ale. As she was coming home, with her ale in a greybeard[2] in her hand, a chaise in full bir[3] came upon her and knocked her down, and broke the greybeard and spilt the liquor. The cry was terrible; some thought poor Peggy was killed outright, and wives, with candles in their hands, started out at the doors and windows. Peggy, however, was more terrified than damaged; but the gentry that were in the chaise, being termagant English travellers, swore like dragoons, that the streets should be indicted as a nuisance; and when they put up at the inns,[4] two of them came to me, as Provost, to remonstrate on the shameful condition of the pavement, and to lodge in my hands the sum of ten pounds for the behoof of Peggy; the which was greater riches than ever the poor creature thought to attain in this world. Seeing they were gentlemen of a right quality, I did what I could to pacify them, by joining in every thing they said in condemnation of the streets; telling them, at the same time, that the improvement of the causey, was to be the very first object and care of my Provostry. And I bade Mrs. Pawkie bring in the wine decanters, and requested them to sit down with me and take a glass of wine and a sugar-biscuit; the civility of which, on my part, soon brought them into a peaceable way of thinking, and they went away, highly commending my politess and hospitality, of which they spoke in the warmest terms to their companion when they returned to the inns, as the waiter, who attended them, over-heard, and told the landlord, who informed me and others of the same in the morning. So that on the Saturday following, when the town-council met, there was no difficulty in getting a minute entered at the sederunt, that the crown of the causey should be forthwith put in a state of reparation.

Having thus gotten the thing determined upon, I then proposed that we should have the work done by contract, and that notice should be given publicly of such being our intent. Some bogling was made to this proposal, it never having been the use and wont of the corporation, in time past, to do any thing by contract, but just to put whatever was required into the hands of one of the council, who got the work done in the best way he could; by which loose manner of administration great abuses were often allowed to pass unreproved. But I persisted in my resolution to have the causey renewed by contract; and all the inhabitants of the town gave me credit for introducing such a great reformation into the management of public affairs.

When it was made known that we would receive offers to contract, divers persons came forward; and I was a little at a loss, when I saw such competition, as to which ought to be preferred. At last, I bethought me, to send for the different competitors, and converse with them on the subject quietly; and I found, in Thomas Shovel, the tacksman of the Whinstone-quarry,[1] a discreet and considerate man. His offer was, it is true, not so low as some of the others; but he had facilities to do the work quickly, that none of the rest could pretend to; so, upon a clear understanding of that, with the help of Dean of Guild M'Lucre's advocacy, Thomas Shovel got the contract. At first, I could not divine what interest my old friend, the Dean of Guild, had to be so earnest in the behalf of the offering contractor; in course of time, however, it spunkit[2] out, that he was a sleeping partner in the business; by which he made a power of profit. But, saving two three carts of stones to big a dyke[3] round the new steading which I had bought a short time before at the townend, I had no benefit whatever. Indeed, I may take it upon me to say, that should not say it, few Provosts, in so great a concern, could have acted more on a principle than I did in this; and if Thomas Shovel, of his free-will, did, at the instigation of the Dean of Guild, lay down the stones on my ground as aforesaid, the town was not wronged; for, no doubt, he paid me the compliment at some expense of his own profit.

CHAPTER XVI

THE REPAIR OF THE KIRK

THE repair of the kirk, the next job I took in hand, was not so easily managed as that of the causey; for it seems, in former times, the whole space of the area had been free to the parish in general; and that the lofts[1] were constructions, raised at the special expence of the heritors for themselves. The fronts being for their families, and the back seats for their servants and tenants. In those times, there were no such things as pews; but only forms, removeable, as I have heard say, at pleasure.

It, however, happened, in the course of nature, that certain forms came to be sabbathly frequented by the same persons; who, in this manner, acquired a sort of prescriptive right to them. And those persons or families, one after another, finding it would be an ease and convenience to them during divine worship, put up backs to their forms. But still, for many a year, there was no inclosure of pews; the first, indeed, that made a pew, as I have been told, was one Archibald Rafter, a wright, and the grandfather of Mr. Rafter, the architect, who has had so much to do with the edification[2] of the new town of Edinburgh. This Archibald's form happened to be near the door, on the left-side of the pulpit; and in the winter, when the wind was in the north, it was a very cold seat, which induced him to inclose it round and round, with certain old doors and shutters, which he had acquired in taking down and rebuilding the left-wing of the Whinnyhill-house. The comfort in which this enabled him and his family to listen to the worship, had an immediate effect; and the example being of a taking nature, in the course of little more than twenty years from the time, the whole area of the kirk had been pewed in a very creditable manner.

Families thus getting, as it were, portions of the church, some, when removing from the town, gave them up to their neighbours, on receiving a consideration for the expence they had been at in making the pews; so that, from less to more, the pews so formed became a lettable and a vendible property;[1] it was, therefore, thought a hard thing, that in the reparation which the seats had come to require in my time, the heritors and corporation should be obligated to pay the cost and expence of what was so clearly the property of others; while it seemed an impossibility to get the whole tot of the proprietors of the pews to bear the expence of new-seating the kirk. We had in the council many a long and weighty sederunt on the subject, without coming to any practical conclusion. At last, I thought the best way, as the kirk was really become a disgrace to the town, would be, for the corporation to undertake the repair entirely; upon an understanding, that we were to be paid eighteen-pence a bottom-room *per annum*, by the proprietors of the pews; and, on sounding the heritors, I found them all most willing to consent thereto, glad to be relieved from the awful expence of gutting and replenishing such a great concern as the kirk was. Accordingly, the council having agreed to this proposal, we had plans and estimates made, and notice given to the owners of pews of our intention. The whole proceedings gave the greatest satisfaction possible to the inhabitants in general, who lauded and approved of my discernment more and more.

By the estimate, it was found, that the repairs would cost about a thousand pounds; and by the plan, that the seats, at eighteen-pence a sitter, would yield better than a hundred pounds a year; so that there was no scruple on the part of the town-council, in borrowing the money wanted. This was the first public debt ever contracted by the corporation, and people were very fain to get their money lodged at five per cent. on such good security; in so much, that we had a great deal more offered than we required at that time and epoch.

CHAPTER XVII

THE LAW PLEA

THE repair of the kirk was undertaken by contract with William Plane, the joiner, with whom I was in terms at the time, anent the bigging of a land of houses[1] on my new steading at the town end. A most reasonable man in all things he was, and in no concern of my own had I a better satisfaction than in the house he built for me at the conjuncture[2] when he had the town's work in the kirk; but there was at that period among us a certain person, of the name of Nabal Smeddum, a tobacconist by calling, who, up to this season, had been regarded but as a droll and comical bodie at a coothy crack.[3] He was, in stature, of the lower order of mankind, but endowed with an inclination towards corpulency, by which he had acquired some show of a belly, and his face was round, and his cheeks both red and sleeky. He was, however, in his personalities, chiefly remarkable for two queer and twinkling little eyes, and for a habitual custom of licking his lips whenever he said any thing of pith or jocossity, or thought that he had done so, which was very often the case. In his apparel, as befitted his trade, he wore a suit of snuff-coloured cloth, and a brown round-eared wig, that curled close in to his neck.

Mr. Smeddum, as I have related, was in some estimation for his comicality; but he was a dure hand at an argument, and would not see the plainest truth, when it was not on his side of the debate. No occasion or cause however had come to pass, by which this inherent cross-grainedness was stirred into action, till the affair of reseating the kirk, a measure, as I have mentioned, which gave the best satisfaction; but it happened that, on a Saturday night, as I was going soberly home from a meeting of the magistrates in the clerk's chamber, I by chance recollected that I stood in need of having my box replenished; and accordingly, in the most innocent and harmless manner that it was possible for a man to do, I stepped into this Mr. Smeddum, the tobacconist's shop, and while he was compounding my mixture from the two canisters that stood on his counter, and I was in a manner doing nothing, but looking at the number of counterfeit sixpences and shillings that were nailed thereon as an admonishment to his customers, he said to me, 'So, Provost, we're to hae a new lining to the kirk. I wonder, when ye were at it, that ye did na rather think of bigging another frae the fundament,[1] for I'm thinking the walls are no o' a capacity of strength to outlast this seating.'

Knowing, as I did, the tough temper of the bodie, I can attribute my entering into an argument with him on the subject, to nothing but some inconsiderate infatuation; for when I said, heedlessly, the walls are very good, he threw the brass snuff-spoon with an ecstacy into one of the canisters, and lifting his two hands into a posture of admiration, cried as if he had seen an unco[2]——

'Good! surely, Provost, ye hae na had an inspection— they're crackit in divers places; they're shotten out wi' infirmity in others; in short, the whole kirk, frae the coping to the fundament, is a fabric smitten wi' a paralytic.'

'It's very extraordinar, Mr. Smeddum,' was my reply, 'that nobody has seen a' this but yoursel.'

'Na, if ye will deny the fact, Provost,' quo' he, 'it's o' no service for me to say a word; but there has to a moral certainty been a slackness somewhere, or how has it happened that the wa's were na subjected to a right inspection before this job o' the seating?'

By this time I had seen the great error into the which I had fallen, by entering on a confabulation with Mr. Smeddum; so I said to him, 'It's no a matter for you and me to dispute about, so I'll thank you to fill my box;' the which manner of putting an end to the debate he took very ill, and after I left the shop, he laid the marrow of our discourse open to Mr. Threeper, the writer,[1] who by chance went in, like mysel, to get a supply of rappee for the Sabbath. That limb of the law discerning a sediment of litigation in the case, eggit on Mr. Smeddum into a persuasion, that the seating of the kirk was a thing which the magistrates had no legal authority to undertake. At this critical moment, my ancient adversary and seeming friend, the Dean of Guild, happened to pass the door, and the bickering snuff-man seeing him, cried[2] to him to come in. It was a very unfortunate occurrence; for Mr. M'Lucre, having a secret interest, as I have intimated, in the Whinstone quarry, when he heard of taking down walls and bigging them up again, he listened with greedy ears to the dubieties of Mr. Threeper, and loudly, and to the heart's content of Mr. Smeddum, condemned the frailty and infirmity of the kirk, as a building in general.

It would be overly tedious to mention, however, all the outs and inns of the affair; but from less to more, a faction was begotten, and grew to head, and stirring among the inhabitants of the town, not only with regard to the putting of new seats within the old walls, but likewise as to the power of the magistrates to lay out any part of the public funds in the reparation of the kirk; and the upshot was, a contribution among certain malcontents to enable Mr. Threeper to consult counsel on all the points.

As, in all similar cases, the parties applying for legal advice were heartened into a plea by the opinion they got, and the town-council was thrown into the greatest consternation by receiving notice that the malcontents were going to extremities.

Two things I saw it was obligational on me to urge forward; the one was to go on still with the reparations, and the other to contest the law-suit, although some were for waiting in the first case till the plea was settled, and in the second to make no defence, but to give up our intention anent the new-seating. But I thought, that, as we had borrowed the money for the repairs, we should proceed; and I had a vista that the contribution raised by the Smeddumites, as they were called, would run out, being from their own pockets, whereas we fought with the public purse in our hand, and by dint of exhortation to that effect, I carried the majority to go into my plan, which in the end was most gratifying, for the kirk was in a manner made as good as new, and the contributional stock of the Smeddumites was entirely rookit[1] by the lawyers, who would fain have had them to form another, assuring them that, no doubt, the legal point was in their favour. But every body knows the uncertainty of a legal opinion, and although the case was given up, for lack of a fund to carry it on, there was a living ember of discontent left in its ashes, ready to kindle into a flame on the first puff of popular dissatisfaction.

CHAPTER XVIII

THE SUPPRESSION OF THE FAIRS

THE spirit by which the Smeddumites were actuated in ecclesiastical affairs, was a type and taste of the great distemper with which all the world was, more or less, at the time inflamed, and which cast the ancient state and monarchy of France into the perdition of anarchy and confusion. I think, upon the whole, however, that our royal borough was not afflicted to any very dangerous degree, though there was a sort of itch of it among a few of the sedentary orders, such as the weavers and shoemakers, who, by the nature of sitting long in one posture, are apt to become subject to the flatulence of theoretical opinions; but although this was my notion, yet knowing how much better the king and government were acquainted with the true condition of things, than I could to a certainty be, I kept a steady eye on the proceedings of the ministers and parliament at London, taking them for an index and model for the management of the public concerns, which, by the grace of God, and the handling of my friends, I was raised up and set forward to undertake.

Seeing the great dread and anxiety that was above, as to the inordinate liberty of the multitude, and how necessary it was to bridle popularity, which was become rampant and ill to ride, kicking at all established order, and trying to throw both king and nobles from the saddle, I resolved to discountenance all tumultuous meetings, and to place every reasonable impediment in the way of multitudes assembling together; indeed, I had for many years been of opinion, that fairs were become a great political evil to the regular shopkeepers, by reason of the packmen, and other travelling merchants, coming with their wares, and underselling us, so that both private interest and public principle incited me on to do all in my power to bring our fair-days into disrepute. It cannot be told what a world of thought and consideration this cost me, before I lighted on the right method, nor, without a dive into the past times of antiquity, is it in the power of man to understand the difficulties of the matter.

Some of our fair-days were remnants of the papistical idolatry, and instituted of old by the Pope and Cardinals, in order to make an income from the vice and immorality that was usually rife at the same. These, in the main points, were only market-days of a blither kind than the common. The country folks came in dressed in their best, the schools got the play, and a long rank of sweety-wives and their stands, covered with the wonted dainties of the occasion, occupied the sunny side of the High-street, while the shady side was, in like manner, taken possession of by the packmen, who, in their booths, made a marvellous display of goods of an inferior quality, with laces and ribbons of all colours, hanging down in front, and twirling like pinnets[1] in the wind. There was likewise the allurement of some compendious show of wild beasts; in short, a swatch of everything that the art of man has devised for such occasions, to wile away the bawbee.

Besides the fairs of this sort, that may be said to be of a pious origin, there were others of a more boisterous kind, that had come of the times of trouble, when the trades paraded with warlike weapons, and the banners of their respective crafts, and in every seventh year we had a resuscitation of king Crispianus in all his glory and regality, with the man in the coat of mail, of bell-metal, and the dukes, and Lord Mayor of London, at the which, the influx of lads and lasses from the country was just prodigious, and the rioting and rampaging at night, the brulies[1] and the dancing, was worse than Vanity Fair in the Pilgrim's Progress.

To put down, and utterly to abolish, by stress of law, or authority, any ancient pleasure of the commonality, I had learnt, by this time, was not wisdom, and that the fairs were only to be effectually suppressed by losing their temptations, and so to cease to call forth any expectation of merriment among the people. Accordingly, with respect to the fairs of pious origin, I, without expounding my secret motives, persuaded the council, that, having been at so great an expence in new-paving the streets, we ought not to permit the heavy caravans of wild beasts to occupy, as formerly, the front of the Tolbooth towards the cross; but order them, for the future, to keep at the Greenhead.[2] This was, in a manner, expurgating them out of the town altogether; and the consequence was, that the people, who were wont to assemble in the High-street, came to be divided, part gathering at the Greenhead, round the shows, and part remaining among the stands and the booths; thus an appearance was given of the fairs being less attended than formerly, and gradually, year after year, the venerable race of sweetie wives, and chatty packmen, that were so detrimental to the shop-keepers, grew less and less numerous, until the fairs fell into insignificance.

At the parade fair, the remnant of the weapon-showing, I proceeded more roundly to work, and resolved to debar, by proclamation, all persons from appearing with arms; but the deacons of the trades spared me the trouble of issuing the same, for they dissuaded their crafts from parading. Nothing, however, so well helped me out, as the volunteers, of which I will speak by and bye; for when the war began, and they were formed, nobody could afterwards abide to look at the fantastical and disorderly marching of the trades, in their processions and paradings; so that, in this manner, all the glory of the fairs being shorn and expunged, they have fallen into disrepute, and have suffered a natural suppression.

CHAPTER XIX

THE VOLUNTEERING

THE volunteers began in the year 1793, when the democrats in Paris threatened the downfal and utter subversion of kings, lords, and commons. As became us who were of the council, we drew up an address to his Majesty, assuring him that our lives and fortunes were at his disposal. To the which dutiful address, we received, by return of post, a very gracious answer, and, at the same time, the lord-lieutenant gave me a bit hint, that it would be very pleasant to his Majesty, to hear that we had volunteers[1] in our town, men of creditable connections, and willing to defend their property.

When I got this note from his lordship, I went to Mr. Pipe, the wine-merchant, and spoke to him concerning it, and we had some discreet conversation on the same; in the which it was agreed between us, that as I was now rather inclined to a corpulency of parts, and being likewise chief civil magistrate, it would not do to set myself at the head of a body of soldiers, but that the consequence might be made up to me in the clothing of the men; so I consented to put the business into his hands upon this understanding. Accordingly, he went the same night with me to Mr. Dinton that was in the general merchandizing line, a part-owner in vessels, a trafficker in corn, and now and then a canny[1] discounter of bills, at a moderate rate, to folk in straits and difficulties. And we told him,—the same being agreed between us, as the best way of fructifying the job to a profitable issue,—that, as Provost, I had got an intimation to raise a corps of volunteers, and that I thought no better hand could be got for a co-operation than him and Mr. Pipe, who was pointed out to me, as a gentleman weel qualified for the command.

Mr. Dinton, who was a proud man, and an offset from one of the county families, I could see, was not overly pleased at the preferment over him given to Mr. Pipe, so that I was in a manner constrained to loot a sort a-jee,[2] and to wile him into good-humour with all the ability in my power, by saying that it was natural enough of the king and government to think of Mr. Pipe, as one of the most proper men in the town, he paying, as he did, the largest sum of the King's dues at the excise, and being, as we all knew, in a great correspondence with foreign ports—and I winkit to Mr. Pipe, as I said this, and he could with a difficulty keep his countenance at hearing how I so beguiled Mr. Dinton into a spirit of loyalty for the raising of the volunteers.

The ice being thus broken, next day we had a meeting, before the council met, to take the business into public consideration, and we thereat settled on certain creditable persons in the town, of a known principle, as the fittest to be officers under the command of Mr. Pipe, as commandant, and Mr. Dinton, as his colleague under him. We agreed among us, as the custom was in other places, that they should be elected Major, Captain, Lieutenants, and Ensigns, by the free votes of the whole corps, according to the degrees that we had determined for them. In the doing of this, and the bringing it to pass, my skill and management was greatly approved and extolled by all who had a peep behind the curtain.

The town-council being, as I have intimated, convened to hear the gracious answer to the address read, and to take into consideration the suggesting anent the volunteering, met in

the clerk's chamber, where we agreed to call a meeting of
the inhabitants of the town, by proclamation, and by notice
in the church. This being determined, Mr. Pipe and Mr.
Dinton got a paper drawn up, and, privately, before the
Sunday, a number of their genteeler friends, including those
whom we had noted down to be elected officers, set their
names as willing to be volunteers.

On the Sunday, Mr. Pittle, at my instigation, preached a
sermon, showing forth the necessity of arming ourselves in
the defence of all that was dear to us. It was a discourse of great
method, and sound argument, but not altogether so quickened
with pith and bir as might have been wished for; but it paved
the way to the reading out of the summons for the inhabitants
to meet the magistrates in the church, on the Thursday
following, for the purpose, as it was worded by the town-clerk,
to take into consideration the best means of saving the king
and kingdom in the then monstrous crisis of public affairs.

The discourse, with the summons, and a rumour and
whispering that had in the meantime taken place, caused the
desired effect; in so much, that, on the Thursday, there was a
great congregation of the male portion of the people. At the
which, old Mr. Dravel, a genteel man he was, well read in
matters of history, though somewhat overportioned with a
conceit of himself, got up on the table, in one of the table-seats
forenent[1] the pu'pit, and made a speech suitable to the
occasion; in the which he set forth what manful things had
been done of old by the Greeks and the Romans for their
country, and, waxing warm with his subject, he cried out with
a loud voice, towards the end of the discourse, giving at the
same time a stamp with his foot, 'Come, then, as men and as
citizens; the cry is for your altars and your God.'

'Gude saves,[2] Mr. Dravel, are ye gane by yoursel?' cried
Willy Coggle, from the front of the loft, a daft bodie that was
ay far ben on all public occasions—'to think that our God's a
Pagan image in need of sick feckless[3] help as the like o' thine.'
The which outcry of Willy raised a most extraordinary laugh

at the fine paternoster, about the ashes of our ancestors, that
Mr. Dravel had been so vehemently rehearsing; and I was
greatly afraid, that the solemnity of the day would be turned
into a ridicule. However, Mr. Pipe, who was upon the whole a
man no without both sense and capacity, rose, and said, that
our business was to strengthen the hands of government, by
coming forward as volunteers; and therefore, without thinking it necessary among the people of this blessed land, to
urge any arguments in furtherance of that object, he would
propose that a volunteer corps should be raised; and he
begged leave of me, who, as Provost, was in the chair, to read a
few words that he had hastily thrown together on the subject,
as the outlines of a pact of agreement among those who might
be inclined to join with him. I should here, however, mention,
that the said few words of a pact was the costive product
overnight of no small endeavour between me and Mr. Dinton
as well as him.

When he had thus made his motion, Mr. Dinton, as we
had concerted, got up and seconded the same, pointing out the
liberal spirit in which the agreement was drawn, as every
person signing it was eligible to be an officer of any rank, and
every man had a vote in the preferment of the officers. All
which was mightily applauded; and upon this I rose, and said,
'It was a pleasant thing for me to have to report to his
Majesty's government, the loyalty of the inhabitants of our
town, and the unanimity of the volunteering spirit among
them,—and to testify,' said I, 'to all the world, how much we
are sensible of the blessings of the true liberty we enjoy, I
would suggest, that the matter of the volunteering be left
entirely to Mr. Pipe and Mr. Dinton, with a few other
respectable gentlemen, as a committee, to carry the same into
effect;' and with that I looked, as it were, round the church,
and then said, 'There's Mr. Oranger, a better could na be
joined with them.' He was a most creditable man, and a
grocer, that we had waled[1] out for a captain; so I desired,
having got a nod of assent from him, that Mr. Oranger's

name might be added to their's, as one of the committee. In like manner I did by all the rest whom we had previously chosen. Thus, in a manner, predisposing the public towards them for officers.

In the course of the week, by the endeavours of the committee, a sufficient number of names was got to the paper, and the election of the officers came on, on the Tuesday following; at which, though there was a sort of a contest, and nothing could be a fairer election, yet the very persons that we had chosen were elected, though some of them had but a narrow chance. Mr. Pipe was made the commandant, by a superiority of only two votes, over Mr. Dinton.

CHAPTER XX

THE CLOTHING

IT was an understood thing, at first, that, saving in the matter of guns and other military implements, the volunteers were to be at all their own expences; out of which, both tribulation and disappointment ensued; for when it came to be determined about the uniforms, Major Pipe found that he could by no possibility wise[1] all the furnishing to me, every one being disposed to get his regimentals from his own merchant; and there was also a division anent the colour of the same, many of the doucer sort of the men being blate[2] of appearing in scarlet and gold-lace, insisting, with a great earnestness, almost to a sedition, on the uniform being blue. So that the whole advantage of a contract was frustrated, and I began to be sorry that I had not made a point of being, notwithstanding the alleged weight and impediment of my corpulence, the Major-commandant myself. However, things, after some time, began to take a turn for the better; and the art of raising volunteers being better understood in the kingdom, Mr. Pipe went into Edinburgh, and upon some conference with the Lord Advocate, got permission to augment his force by another company, and leave to draw two days' pay a week, for account of the men, and to defray the necessary expences of the corps. The doing of this bred no little agitation in the same; and some of the forward and upsetting spirits of the younger privates that had been smitten, though not in a disloyal sense, with the insubordinate spirit of the age, clamoured about the rights of the original bargain with them, insisting, that the officers had no privilege to sell their independence, and a deal of trash of that sort, and finally withdrew from the corps, drawing, to the consternation of the officers, the pay that had been taken in their names; and which the officers could not refuse, although it was really wanted for the contingencies of the service, as Major Pipe himself told me.

When the corps had thus been rid of these turbulent spirits, the men grew more manageable and rational, assenting, by little and little, to all the proposals of the officers, until there was a true military dominion of discipline gained over them; and a joint contract was entered into, between Major Pipe and me, for a regular supply of all necessaries, in order to insure a uniform appearance, which, it is well known, is essential to a right discipline. In the end, when the eyes of men in civil stations had got accustomed to military show and parade, it was determined to change the colour of the cloth from blue to red, the former having at first been preferred, and worn for some time; in the accomplishment of which change, I had (and why should I disguise the honest fact) my share of the advantage which the kingdom at large drew, in that period of anarchy and confusion, from the laudable establishment of a volunteer force.

CHAPTER XXI

THE PRESS-GANG

DURING the same just and necessary war for all that was dear to us, in which the volunteers were raised, one of the severest trials happened to me that ever any magistrate was subjected to. I had, at the time, again subsided into an ordinary counsellor, but it so fell out, that by reason of Mr. Shuttle-thrift, who was then provost, having occasion and need to go into Glasgow upon some affairs of his own private concerns, he being interested in the Kilbeacon Cotton Mill,[1] and Mr. Dalrye, the bailie, who should have acted for him being like-wise from home, anent a plea he had with a neighbour concerning the bounds of their rigs and gables,[2] the whole authority and power of the magistrates devolved, by a courtesy on the part of their colleague Bailie Hammerman, into my hands.

For some time before, there had been an in-gathering among us of sailor lads from the neighbouring ports, who, on their arrival, in order to shun the press-gangs, left their vessels, and came to scog[3] themselves with us. By this a rumour or a suspicion rose, that the men-of-wars-men were suddenly to come at the dead hour of the night and sweep them all away. Heaven only knows, whether this notice was bred in the fears and jealousies[4] of the people, or was a humane inkling given by some of the men-of-wars-men, to put the poor sailor lads on their guard, was never known. But, on a Saturday night, as I was on the eve of stepping into my bed, I shall never forget it, Mrs. Pawkie was already in and as sound as a door-nail, and I was just crooking my mouth to blow out the candle, when I heard a rap. As our bed-room window was over the door, I looked out. It was a dark night, but I could see by a glaike of light from a neighbour's window that there was a man with a cocked hat at the door.

'What's your will?' said I to him, as I looked out at him in my night-cap. He made no other answer, but that he was one of his Majesty's officers, and had business with the justice.

I did not like this Englification and voice of claim and authority; however, I drew on my stockings and breeks again, and taking my wife's flannel coaty about my shoulders, for I was then troubled with the rheumatise, I went down, and, opening the door, let in the lieutenant.

'I come,' said he, 'to show you my warrant and commission, and to acquaint you, that having information of several able-bodied seamen being in the town, I mean to make a search for them.'

I really did not well know what to say at the moment; but I begged him, for the love of peace and quietness, to defer his work till the next morning; but he said he must obey his orders, and he was sorry that it was his duty to be on so disagreeable a service, with many other things, that showed something like a sense of compassion, that could not have been hoped for in the captain of a press-gang.

When he had said this, he then went away, saying, for he saw my tribulation, that it would be as well for me to be prepared in case of any riot. This was the worst news of all; but what could I do? I thereupon went again to Mrs. Pawkie, and shaking her awake, told her what was going on, and a terrified woman she was. I then dressed myself with all possible expedition, and went to the town clerk's, and we sent for the town-officers, and then adjourned to the council-chamber, to wait the issue of what might betide.

In my absence, Mrs. Pawkie rose out of her bed, and by some wonderful instinct, collecting all the bairns, went with them to the minister's house, as to a place of refuge and sanctuary.

Shortly after we had been in the council room, I opened the window, and looked out, but all was still; the town was lying in the defencelessness of sleep, and nothing was heard but the clicking of the town-clock in the steeple over our heads. By and bye, however, a sough and pattering of feet was heard approaching; and shortly after, in looking out, we saw the press-gang, headed by their officers, with cutlasses by their side, and great club-sticks in their hands. They said nothing, but the sound of their feet on the silent stones of the causey was as the noise of a dreadful engine. They passed, and went on; and all that were with me in the council stood at the windows, and listened. In the course of a minute or two after, two lassies, with a callan,[1] that had been out, came flying and wailing, giving the alarm to the town. Then we heard the driving of the bludgeons on the doors, and the outcries of terrified women; and, presently after, we saw the poor chased sailors running, in their shirts, with their clothes in their hands, as if they had been felons and blackguards caught in guilt, and flying from the hands of justice.

The town was awakened with the din, as with the cry of fire; and lights came starting forward, as it were, to the windows. The women were out with lamentations and vows of vengeance. I was in a state of horror unspeakable. Then came some three or four of the press-gang, with a struggling sailor in their clutches, with nothing but his trowsers on, his shirt riven from his back in the fury. Syne came the rest of the gang, and their officers, scattered, as it were, with a tempest of mud and stones, pursued and battered by a troop of desperate women and weans,[2] whose fathers and brothers were in jeopardy. And these were followed by the wailing wife of the pressed man, with her five bairns, clamouring in their agony to Heaven against the king and government for the outrage. I could na listen to the fearful justice of their outcry; but sat down in a corner of the council-chamber, with my fingers in my ears.

In a little while, a shout of triumph rose from the mob, and we heard them returning, and I felt, as it were, relieved; but the sound of their voices became hoarse and terrible as they drew near; and, in a moment, I heard the jingle of twenty broken windows rattle in the street. My heart misgave me; and, indeed, it was my own windows. They left not one pane unbroken; and nothing kept them from demolishing the house to the ground-stone but the exhortations of Major Pipe; who, on hearing the uproar, was up and out; and did all in his power to arrest the fury of the tumult. It seems, the mob had taken it into their heads that I had signed, what they called the press-warrants; and, on driving the gang out of the town, and rescuing the man, they came to revenge themselves on me and mine; which is the cause, that made me say, it was a miraculous instinct that led Mrs. Pawkie to take the family to Mr. Pittle's; for had they been in the house, it is not to be told what the consequences might have been.

Before morning the riot was ended; but the damage to my house was very great; and I was intending, as the public had done the deed, that the town should have paid for it. 'But,' said Mr. Keelivine, the town-clerk, 'I think you may do better; and this calamity, if properly handled to the government, may make your fortune.' I reflected on the hint; and, accordingly, the next day, I went over to the regulating Captain of the press-gang, and represented to him the great damage and detriment which I had suffered; requesting him to represent to government, that it was all owing to the part I had taken in his behalf. To this, for a time, he made some scruple of objection; but, at last, he drew up, in my presence, a letter to the lords of the Admiralty; telling what he had done, and how he and his men had been ill-used; and, that the house of the chief-magistrate of the town, had been in a manner destroyed by the rioters.

By the same post, I wrote off myself to the Lord Advocate, and likewise to the Secretary of State, in London; commending, very properly, the prudent and circumspect manner in which the officer had come to apprize me of his duty, and giving as faithful an account as I well could of the riot; concluding, with a simple notification of what had been done to my house, and the outcry that might be raised in the town were any part of the town's funds to be used in the repairs.

Both the Lord Advocate and Mr. Secretary of State wrote me back by retour of post, thanking me for my zeal in the public service; and I was informed, that as it might not be expedient to agitate in the town the payment of the damage which my house had received, the Lords of the Treasury would indemnify me for the same; and this was done in a manner which showed the blessings we enjoy, under our most venerable constitution; for I was not only thereby enabled, by what I got, to repair the windows, but to build up a vacant steading;[1] the same, which I settled last year on my dochter, Marion, when she was married to Mr. Geery, of the Gatherton Holme.

CHAPTER XXII

THE WIG DINNER

THE affair of the press-gang gave great concern to all of the council; for it was thought that the loyalty of the borough would be called in question, and doubted by the King's ministers, notwithstanding our many assurances to the contrary;[2] the which sense and apprehension begat among us an inordinate anxiety to manifest our principles on all expedient occasions. In the doing of this, divers curious and comical things came to pass; but the most comical of all was what happened at the Michaelmas dinner[3] following the riot.

The weather, for some days before, had been raw for that time of the year, and Michaelmas-day was, both for wind, and wet, and cold, past ordinar; in so much, that we were obligated to have a large fire in the council-chamber, where we dined. Round this fire, after drinking His Majesty's health and the other appropriate toasts, we were sitting as cozy as could be; and every one the longer he sat, and the oftener his glass visited the punch-bowl, waxed more and more royal, till every body was in a most hilarious temperament, singing songs, and joining chorus with the greatest cordiality.

It happened, among others of the company, there was a gash old carl,[1] the Laird of Bodletonbrae, who was a very capital hand at a joke; and he, chancing to notice that the whole of the magistrates and town-council, then present, wore wigs, feigned to become out of all bounds, with the demonstrations of his devotion to King and country; and others that were there, not wishing to appear any thing behind him in the same, vied in their sprose[2] of patriotism, and bragging in a manful manner of what, in the hour of trial, they would be seen to do. Bodletonbrae was all the time laughing in his sleeve at the way he was working them on, till at last, after they had flung the glasses twice or thrice over their shoulders, he proposed we should throw our wigs in the fire next. Surely there was some glammer[3] about us, that caused us not to observe his devilry, for the laird had no wig on his head. Be that, however, as it may, the instigation took effect, and, in the twinkling of an eye, every scalp was bare, and the chimlay roaring with the roasting of gude kens how many powdered wigs well fattened with pomatum. But scarcely was the deed done, till every one was admonished of his folly, by the laird laughing, like a being out of his senses, at the number of bald heads and shaven crowns that his device had brought to light, and by one and all of us experiencing the coldness of the air on the nakedness of our upper parts.

The first thing that we then did was to send the town-officers, who were waiting on as usual for the dribbles of the bottles and the leavings in the bowls, to bring our night-caps; but I trew[4] few were so lucky as me, for I had a spare wig at home, which Mrs. Pawkie, my wife, a most considerate woman, sent to me; so that I was, in a manner, to all visibility, none the worse of the ploy, but the rest of the council were perfect oddities in their wigs, and the sorest thing of all was that the exploit of burning the wigs had got wind, so that,

when we left the council-room, there was a great congregation
of funny weans and misleart trades-lads[1] assembled before
the tolbooth, shouting, and like as if they were out of the body
with daffing,[2] to see so many of the heads of the town in their
nightcaps, and no, may be, just so solid at the time as could
have been wished. Nor did the matter rest here, for the
generality of the sufferers being in a public way, were obligated to appear the next day in their shops, and at their call-
ings, with their night-caps, for few of them had two wigs like
me, by which no small merriment ensued, and was continued
for many a day. It would hardly, however, be supposed, that,
in such a matter, any thing could have redounded to my
advantage; but so it fell out, that by my wife's prudence in
sending me my other wig, it was observed by the commonality,
when we sallied forth to go home, that I had on my wig, and it
was thought I had a very meritorious command of myself, and
was the only man in the town fit for a magistrate; for in every
thing I was seen to be most cautious and considerate. I could
not, however, when I saw the turn the affair took to my
advantage, but reflect on what small and visionary grounds
the popularity of public men will sometimes rest.

CHAPTER XXIII

THE DEATH OF MR. M'LUCRE

SHORTLY after the affair recorded in the foregoing chapter,
an event came to pass in the borough that had been for some
time foreseen.

My old friend and adversary, Bailie M'Lucre, being now a
man well stricken in years, was one night in going home from
a gavawlling[3] with some of the neighbours at Mr. Shuttle-
thrift's, the manufacturer's, (the Bailie, canny man, never
liket ony thing of the sort at his own cost and outlay,) having

partaken largely of the bowl, for the manufacturer was of a
blithe humour—the Bailie, as I was saying, in going home,
was overtaken by an apoplexy just at the threshold of his own
door, and although it did not kill him outright, it shoved him,
as it were, almost into the very grave; in so much, that he never
spoke an articulate word during the several weeks he was
permitted to doze away his latter end; and accordingly he
died, and was buried in a very creditable manner to the community, in consideration of the long space of time he had been
a public man among us.

But what rendered the event of his death, in my opinion,
the more remarkable, was, that I considered with him the last
remnant of the old practice of managing the concerns of the
town came to a period. For now that he is dead and gone, and
also all those whom I found conjunct with him, when I came
into power and office, I may venture to say, that things in yon
former times were not guided so thoroughly by the hand of a
disinterested integrity as in these latter years. On the contrary,
it seemed to be the use and wont of men in public trusts, to
think they were free to indemnify themselves in a left-handed
way, for the time and trouble they bestowed in the same. But
the thing was not so far wrong in principle, as in the hugger-
muggering way in which it was done, and which gave to it a
guilty colour, that by the judicious stratagem of a right
system, it would never have had. In sooth, to say, through the
whole course of my public life, I met with no greater difficulties and trials, than in cleansing myself from the old
habitudes of office. For I must, in verity, confess, that I myself
partook, in a degree, at my beginning, of the caterpillar[1]
nature; and it was not until the light of happier days called
forth the wings of my endowment, that I became conscious
of being raised into public life for a better purpose than to prey
upon the leaves and flourishes[2] of the commonwealth. So that,
if I have seemed to speak lightly of those doings, that are now
denominated corruptions, I hope it was discerned therein,
that I did so, rather to intimate that such things were, than to

consider them as in themselves commendable. Indeed, in thir[1] notations, I have endeavoured, in a manner, to be governed by the spirit of the times in which the transactions happened, for I have lived long enough to remark, that if we judge of past events by present motives, and do not try to enter into the spirit of the age when they took place, and to see them with the eyes with which they were really seen, we shall conceit many things to be of a bad and wicked character, that were not thought so harshly of by those who witnessed them, nor even by those who, perhaps, suffered from them; while, therefore, I think it has been of a great advantage to the public to have survived that method of administration in which the like of Bailie M'Lucre was engendered, I would not have it understood that I think the men who held the public trusts in those days a whit less honest than the men of my own time. The spirit of their own age was upon them, as that of ours is upon us, and their ways of working the wherry entered more or less into all their trafficking, whether for the commonality, or for their own particular behoof and advantage.

I have been thus large and frank in my reflections anent the death of the Bailie, because, poor man, he had outlived the times for which he was qualified; and instead of the merriment and jocularity that his wily by-hand[2] ways used to cause among his neighbours, the rising generation began to pick and dab at him, in such a manner, that, had he been much longer spared, it is to be feared he would not have been allowed to enjoy his earnings both with ease and honour. However, he got out of the world with some respect, and the matters of which I have now to speak, are exalted, both in method and principle, far above the personal considerations that took something from the public virtue of his day and generation.

CHAPTER XXIV

THE WINDY YULE

I T was in the course of the winter, after the decease of Bailie M'Lucre, that the great loss of lives took place, which every body agreed was one of the most calamitous things that had for many a year befallen the town.

Three or four vessels were coming with cargoes of grain from Ireland; another from the Baltic, with Norawa deals;[1] and a third from Bristol, where she had been on a charter for some Greenock merchants.

It happened that, for a time, there had been contrary winds, against which no vessel could enter the port, and the ships, whereof I have been speaking, were all lying together at anchor in the bay, waiting a change of weather. These five vessels were owned among ourselves, and their crews consisted of fathers and sons belonging to the place, so that both by reason of interest and affection, a more than ordinary concern was felt for them; for the sea was so rough, that no boat could live in it to go near them, and we had our fears that the men on board would be very ill off. Nothing, however, occurred, but this natural anxiety, till the Saturday, which was Yule. In the morning, the weather was blasty and sleety, waxing more and more tempestuous, till about mid-day, when the wind checked suddenly round from the nor-east to the sou-west, and blew a gale, as if the prince of the powers of the air was doing his utmost to work mischief. The rain blattered, the windows clattered, the shop-shutters flapped, pigs from the lum-heads[2] came rattling down like thunder-claps, and the skies were dismal both with cloud and carry.[3] Yet, for all that, there was in the streets a stir and a busy visitation between neighbours, and every one went to their high windows, to look at the five poor barks, that were warsling[4] against the strong arm of the elements of the storm and the ocean.

Still the lift[1] gloomed, and the wind roared, and it was as doleful a sight as ever was seen in any town afflicted with calamity, to see the sailors' wives, with their red cloaks about their heads, followed by their hirpling[2] and disconsolate bairns, going one after another to the kirkyard, to look at the vessels[3] where their helpless breadwinners were battling with the tempest. My heart was really sorrowful, and full of a sore anxiety to think of what might happen to the town, whereof so many were in peril, and to whom no human magistracy could extend the arm of protection. Seeing no abatement of the wrath of heaven, that howled and roared around us, I put on my big coat, and taking my staff in my hand, having tied down my hat with a silk handkerchief, towards gloaming I walked likewise to the kirkyard, where I beheld such an assemblage of sorrow, as few men in situation have ever been put to the trial to witness.

In the lea of the kirk many hundreds of the town were gathered together; but there was no discourse among them. The major part were sailors' wives and weans, and at every new thud of the blast, a sob rose, and the mothers drew their bairns closer in about them, as if they saw the visible hand of a foe raised to smite them. Apart from the multitude, I observed three or four young lasses, standing behind the Whinnyhill families' tomb, and I jealoused that they had joes[4] in the ships, for they often looked to the bay, with long necks and sad faces, from behind the monument. A widow woman, one old Mary Weery, that was a lameter,[5] and dependent on her son, who was on board the Louping Meg, (as the Lovely Peggy was nick-named at the shore,) stood by herself, and every now and then wrung her hands, crying, with a woeful voice, 'The Lord giveth, and the Lord taketh away, blessed be the name of the Lord;'—but it was manifest to all, that her faith was fainting within her. But of all the piteous objects there, on that doleful evening, none troubled my thoughts more than three mother-less children, that belonged to the mate of one of the vessels in the jeopardy. He was an Englishman that had been settled some years in the town, where his family had neither kith nor kin; and his wife having died about a month before, the bairns, of whom the eldest was but nine or so, were friendless enough, though both my gude-wife, and other well-disposed ladies, paid them all manner of attention, till their father would come home. The three poor little things, knowing that he was in one of the ships, had been often out and anxious, and they were then sitting under the lea of a headstone, near their mother's grave, chittering and creeping closer and closer at every squall. Never was such an orphan-like sight seen.

When it began to be so dark, that the vessels could no longer be discerned from the churchyard, many went down to the shore, and I took the three babies home with me, and Mrs. Pawkie made tea for them, and they soon began to play with our own younger children, in blythe forgetfulness of the storm; every now and then, however, the eldest of them, when the shutters rattled, and the lum-head roared, would pause in his innocent daffing, and cower in towards Mrs. Pawkie, as if he was daunted and dismayed by something he knew not what.

Many a one that night walked the sounding shore in sorrow, and fires were lighted along it to a great extent, but the darkness and the noise of the raging deep, and the howling wind, never intermitted till about midnight; at which time a message was brought to me, that it might be needful to send a guard of soldiers to the beach, for that broken masts and tackle, had come in, and that surely some of the barks had perished. I lost no time in obeying this suggestion, which was made to me by one of the owners of the Louping Meg; and to show that I sincerely sympathised with all those in affliction, I rose and dressed myself, and went down to the shore, where I directed several old boats to be drawn up by the fires, and blankets to be brought, and cordials prepared, for them that might be spared with life to reach the land; and I walked the beach with the mourners till the morning.

As the day dawned, the wind began to abate in its violence, and to wear away from the sou-west into the norit;[1] but it was soon discovered, that some of the vessels with the corn had perished; for the first thing seen, was a long fringe of tangle and grain, along the line of the highwater mark, and every one strained with greedy and grieved eyes, as the daylight brightened, to discover which had suffered. But I can proceed no farther with the dismal recital of that doleful morning. Let it suffice here to be known, that, through the haze, we at last saw three of the vessels lying on their beam-ends, with their masts broken, and the waves riding like the furious horses of destruction over them. What had become of the other two, was never known; but it was supposed, that they had foundered at their anchors, and that all on board perished.

The day being now Sabbath, and the whole town idle, every body in a manner was down on the beach, to help and mourn as the bodies, one after another, were cast out by the waves. Alas! few were the better of my provident preparation, and it was a thing not to be described, to see, for more than a mile along the coast, the new-made widows and fatherless bairns, mourning and weeping over the corpses of those they loved. Seventeen bodies were, before ten o'clock, carried to the desolated dwellings of their families; and when old Thomas Pull, the betherel,[2] went to ring the bell for public worship, such was the universal sorrow of the town, that Nanse Donsie, an idiot natural, ran up the street to stop him, crying, in the voice of a pardonable desperation, 'Wha, in sic a time, can praise the Lord?'

CHAPTER XXV

THE SUBSCRIPTION

THE calamity of the storm opened and disposed the hearts of the whole town to charity, and it was a pleasure to behold the manner in which the tide of sympathy flowed towards the sufferers. Nobody went to the church in the forenoon, but when I had returned home from the shore, several of the council met at my house, to confer anent the desolation; and it was concerted among us, at my suggestion, that there should be a meeting of the inhabitants called by the magistrates, for the next day, in order to take the public compassion, with the tear in the eye;—which was accordingly done by Mr. Pittle himself from the pulpit, with a few judicious words on the heavy dispensation. And the number of folk that came forward to subscribe was just wonderful. We got well on to a hundred pounds, in the first two hours, besides many a bundle of old clothes. But one of the most remarkable things in the business, was done by Mr. Macandoe. He was, in his original, a lad of the place, who had gone into Glasgow, where he was in a topping line,[1] and happening to be on a visit to his friends at the time, he came to the meeting, and put down his name for twenty guineas, which he gave me in bank notes. A sum of such liberality as had never been given to the town from one individual man, since the mortification[2] of fifty pounds, that we got by the will of Major Bravery, that died in Cheltenham, in England, after making his fortune in India. The sum total of the subscription, when we got My Lord's five-and-twenty guineas, was better than two hundred pounds sterling; for even several of the country gentlemen were very generous contributors, and it is well known that they are not inordinately charitable, especially to town folks; but the distribution of it was no easy task, for it required a discrimination of character as well as of necessities. It was at first proposed to give it over to the session. I knew, however, that, in their hands, it would do no good, for Mr. Pittle, the minister, was a vain sort of a bodie, and easy to be fleeched,[1] and the bold and the bardy,[2] with him, would be sure to come in for a better share than the meek and the modest, who might be in greater want. So I set myself to consider what was the best way of proceeding; and truly, upon reflection, there are few events in my history that I look back upon with more satisfaction, than the part I performed in this matter. For, before going into any division of the money, I proposed that we should allot it to three classes: those who were destitute; those who had some help, but large families; and those to whom a temporality[3] would be sufficient; and that we should make a visitation to the houses of all the sufferers, in order to class them under their proper heads aright. By this method, and together with what I had done personally in the tempest, I got great praise and laud from all reflecting people; and it is not now to be told, what a consolation was brought to many a sorrowful widow, and orphan's heart, by the patience and temperance with which the fund of liberality was distributed; yet because a small sum was reserved, to help some of the more helpless, at another time, and the same was put out to interest in the town's-books, there were not wanting evil-minded persons, who went about whispering calumnious inuendos to my disadvantage; but I know, by this time, the nature of the world, and how impossible it is to reason with such a seven-headed and ten-horned beast as the multitude. So I said nothing; only I got the town-clerk's young man, who acted as clerk to the committee of the subscription, to make out a fair account of the distribution of the money, and to what intent the residue had been placed in the town-treasurer's hands; and this I sent unto a friend in Glasgow to get printed for me, the which he did; and when I got the copies, I directed one to every individual subscriber, and sent the town-drummer an end's errand[4] with them, which was altogether a proceeding of a method and exactness so by common,[1] that it not only quenched the envy of spite utterly out, but contributed more and more to give me weight and authority with the community, until I had the whole sway and mastery of the town.

CHAPTER XXVI

OF THE PUBLIC LAMPS

DEATH is a great reformer of corporate bodies, and we found, now and then, the benefit of his helping hand in our Royal Borough. From the time of my being chosen into the council, and, indeed, for some years before, Mr. Hirple had been a member, but, from some secret and unexpressed under-standing among us, he was never made a bailie; for he was not liked; having none of that furthy[2] and jocose spirit, so be-coming in a magistrate of that degree, and to which the gifts of gravity and formality make but an unsubstantial substitute. He was, on the contrary, a queer and quistical[3] man, of a small stature of body, with an outshot breast, the which, I am inclined to think, was one of the main causes of our never promoting him into the ostensible magistracy; besides, his temper was exceedingly brittle, and in the debates anent the weightiest concerns of the public, he was apt to puff and fiz, and go off with a pluff of anger like a pioye;[4] so that, for the space of more than five-and-twenty years, we would have been glad of his resignation; and, in the heat of argument, there was no lack of hints to that effect from more than one of his friends, especially from Bailie Picken, who was himself a sharp-tempered individual, and could as ill sit quiet under a contradiction as any man I ever was conjunct with. But just before the close of my second provostry, Providence was kind to Mr. Hirple, and removed him gently away from the cares, and troubles, and the vain policy of this contending world, into, as I hope and trust, a far better place.

It may seem, hereafter, to the unlearned readers, among posterity, particularly to such of them as may happen not to be versed in that state of things which we were obligated to endure, very strange that I should make this special mention of Mr. Hirple at his latter end, seeing and observing the small store and account I have thus set upon his talents and personalities. But the verity of the reason is plainly this; we never discovered his worth and value till we had lost him, or rather, till we found the defect and gap that his death caused, and the affliction that came in through it upon us in the ill-advised selection of Mr. Hickery to fill his vacant place.

The spunky[1] nature of Mr. Hirple was certainly very disagreeable often to most of the council, especially when there was any difference of opinion; but then it was only a sort of flash, and at the vote he always, like a reasonable man, sided with the majority, and never after attempted to rip up a decision when it was once so settled. Mr. Hickery was just the even down reverse of this; he never, to be sure, ran himself into a passion, but then he continued to speak and argue so long in reply, never heeding the most rational things of his adversaries, that he was sure to put every other person in a rage; in addition to all which, he was likewise a sorrowful bodie in never being able to understand how a determination by vote ought to and did put an end to every questionable proceeding, so that he was, for a constancy, ever harping about the last subject discussed, as if it had not been decided, until a new difference of opinion arose, and necessitated him to change the burden and o'er-come[2] of his wearysome speeches.

It may seem remarkable that we should have taken such a plague into the council, and be thought that we were well served for our folly; but we were unacquaint with the character of the man—for although a native of the town, he was in truth a stranger, having, at an early age, espoused his fortune, and gone to Philadelphia in America; and no doubt his argolbargolous disposition was an inheritance accumulated with his other conquest of wealth from the mannerless Yankies. Coming home and settling among us, with a power of money, (some said eleven thousand pounds) a short time before Mr. Hirple departed this life, we all thought, on that event happening, it would be a very proper compliment to take Mr. Hickery into the council, and accordingly, we were so misfortunate as to do so; but I trow we soon had reason to repent our indiscretion, and none more than myself, who had first proposed him.

Mr. Hickery having been chosen to supply the void caused by the death of Mr. Hirple, in the very first sederunt of the council after his election, he kithed[1] in his true colours.

Among other things that I had contemplated for the ornament and edification of the borough, was the placing up of lamps[2] to light the streets, such as may be seen in all well regulated cities and towns of any degree. Having spoken of this patriotic project to several of my colleagues, who all highly approved of the same, I had no jealousy or suspicion that a design so clearly and luminously useful would meet with any other opposition than, may be, some doubt as to the fiscal abilities of our income. To be sure Mr. Dribbles, who at that time kept the head inns, and was in the council, said with a wink, that it might be found an inconvenience to sober folk that happened, on an occasion now and then, to be an hour later than usual among their friends, either at his house or any other, to be shown by the lamps to the profane populace as they were making the best of their way home; and Mr. Dippings, the candlemaker, with less public spirit than might have been expected from one who made such a penny by the illuminations on news of victory,[3] was of opinion, that lamps would only encourage the commonality to keep late hours, and that the gentry were in no need of any thing of the sort, having their own handsome glass lanthorns, with two candles in them, garnished and adorned with clippit paper; an equipage which he prophesied would soon wear out of fashion when lamps were once introduced, and the which prediction

I have lived to see verified; for certainly, now-a-days, except when some elderly widow-lady, or maiden gentlewoman, wanting the help and protection of man, happens to be out at her tea and supper, a tight and snod[1] serving lassie, with a three-cornered glass lanthorn, is never seen on the causey. But, to return from this digression; saving and excepting the remarks of Mr. Dribbles and Mr. Dippings, and neither of them could be considered as made in a sincere frame of mind, I had no foretaste of any opposition. I was, therefore, but ill prepared for the worrying argument with which Mr. Hickery seized upon the scheme, asserting and maintaining, among other apparatus-like reasoning, that in such a northern climate as that of Scotland, and where the twilight was of such long duration, it would be a profligate waste of the public money to employ it on any thing so little required as lamps were in our streets.

He had come home from America in the summer time, and I reminded him, that it certainly could never be the intention of the magistrates to light the lamps all the year round, but that in winter there was a great need of them, for in our northern climate, the days were then very short, as he would soon experience, and might probably recollect. But never, surely was such an endless man created. For, upon this, he immediately rejoined, that the streets would be much more effectually lighted, than by all the lamps I proposed to put up, were the inhabitants ordered to sit with their window-shutters open. I really did not know what answer to make to such a proposal, but I saw it would never do to argue with him; so I held my tongue quietly, and as soon as possible, on a pretence of private business, left the meeting, not a little mortified to find such a contrary spirit had got in among us.

After that meeting of the council, I went cannily round to all the other members, and represented to them, one by one, how proper it was that the lamps should be set up, both for a credit to the town, and as a conformity to the fashion of the age in every other place. And I took occasion to descant, at some length, on the untractable nature of Mr. Hickery, and how it would be proper before the next meeting to agree to say nothing when the matter was again brought on the carpet, but just to come to the vote at once. Accordingly this was done, but it made no difference to Mr. Hickery; on the contrary, he said, in a vehement manner, that he was sure there must be some corrupt understanding among us, otherwise a matter of such importance could not have been decided by a silent vote, and at every session of the council, till some new matter of difference cast up, he continued cuckooing about the lamp-job, as he called it, till he had sickened every body out of all patience.

CHAPTER XXVII

THE PLAIN-STONES

THE first question that changed the bark of Mr. Hickery, was my proposal for the side plain-stones[1] of the high street. In the new paving of the crown of the causey, some years before, the rise in the middle had been levelled to an equality with the side loans,[2] and in disposing of the lamp posts, it was thought advantageous to place them half way from the houses and the syvers,[3] between the loans and the crown of the causey which had the effect, at night, of making the people who were wont, in their travels and visitations, to keep the middle of the street, to diverge into the space and path between the lamp-posts and the houses. This, especially in wet weather, was attended with some disadvantages; for the pavement, close to the houses, was not well laid, and there being then no ronns[4] to the houses, at every other place, particularly where the nepus-gables[5] were towards the streets, the rain came gushing in a spout, like as if the windows of heaven were opened. And, in consequence, it began to be freely conversed, that there would be a great comfort in having the sides of the streets paved with flags, like the plain-stones of Glasgow,[1] and that an obligation should be laid on the landlords, to put up ronns, to kepp[2] the rain, and to conduct the water down in pipes by the sides of the houses; —all which furnished Mr. Hickery with fresh topics for his fasherie[3] about the lamps, and was, as he said, proof and demonstration of that most impolitic, corrupt, and short-sighted job, the consequences of which would reach, in the shape of some new tax, every ramification of society;—with divers other American argumentatives to the same effect. However, in process of time, by a judicious handling, and the help of an advantageous free grassum,[4] which we got for some of the town lands from Mr. Shuttlethrift, the manufacturer, who was desirous to build a villa-house,[5] we got the flag-stone part of the project accomplished, and the landlords gradually, of their own free will, put up the ronns, by which the town has been greatly improved and convenienced.

But new occasions call for new laws; the side pavement, concentrating the people, required to be kept cleaner, and in better order, than when the whole width of the street was in use; so that the magistrates were constrained to make regulations concerning the same, and to enact fines and penalties against those who neglected to scrape and wash the plain-stones forenent their houses, and to denounce, in the strictest terms, the emptying of improper utensils on the same, and this, until the people had grown into the habitude of attending to the rules, gave rise to many pleas, and contentious appeals and bickerings, before the magistrates. Among others summoned before me for default, was one Mrs. Fenton, commonly called the Tappit-hen, who kept a small change-house,[6] not of the best repute, being frequented by young men, of a station of life that gave her heart and countenance to be bardy,[7] even to the bailies. It happened that, by some inattention, she had, one frosty morning, neglected to soop her flags,[8] and old Miss Peggy Dainty being early afoot, in passing her door committed a false step, by treading on a bit of a lemon's skin, and her heels flying up, down she fell on her back, at full length, with a great cloyt.[1] Mrs. Fenton, hearing the accident, came running to the door, and seeing the exposure that prejink[2] Miss Peggy had made of herself, put her hands to her sides, and laughed for some time, as if she was by herself.[3] Miss Peggy, being sorely hurt in the hinder parts, summoned Mrs. Fenton before me, where the whole affair, both as to what was seen and heard, was so described, with name and surname, that I could not keep my composure. It was, however, made manifest, that Mrs. Fenton had offended the law,[4] in so much, as her flags had not been swept that morning, and therefore, to appease the offended delicacy of Miss Peggy, who was a most respectable lady in single life, I fined the delinquent, five shillings.

'Mr. Pawkie,' said the latheron,[5] 'I'll no pay't. Whar do ye expek a widow woman like me can get five shillings for ony sic nonsense?'

'Ye must not speak in that manner, honest woman,' was my reply; 'but just pay the fine.'

'In deed and truth, Mr. Pawkie,' quo' she, 'its ill getting a breek off a highlandman. I'll pay no sic thing—five shillings— that's a story!'

I thought I would have been constrained to send her to prison, the woman grew so bold and contumacious, when Mr. Hickery came in, and hearing what was going forward, was evidently working himself up to take the randy's part; but, fortunately, she had a suspicion that all the town-council and magistrates were in league against her, on account of the repute of her house, so that when he enquired of her where she lived, with a view, as I suspect, of interceding, she turned to him, and with a leer and a laugh, said, 'Dear me, Mr. Hickery, I'm sure ye hae nae need to speer[6] that!'

The insinuation set up his birzes;[7] but she bamboozled him with her banter, and raised such a laugh against him, that he was fairly driven from the council room, and I was myself obliged to let her go, without exacting the fine.

Who would have thought, that this affair was to prove to me

the means of an easy riddance of Mr. Hickery? But so it turned out; for whether or not there was any foundation for the traffickings with him, which she pretended, he never could abide to hear the story alluded to, which, when I discerned, I took care, whenever he showed any sort of inclination to molest the council with his propugnacity, to joke him about his bonny sweetheart, 'the Tappit-hen,' and he instantly sang dumb, and quietly slipped away; by which it may be seen how curiously events come to pass, since, out of the very first cause of his thwarting me in the lamps, I found, in process of time, a way of silencing him, far better than any sort of truth or reason.

CHAPTER XXVIII

THE SECOND CROP OF VOLUNTEERS

I HAVE already related, at full length, many of the particulars anent the electing of the first set of volunteers; the which, by being germinated partly under the old system of public intro-mission,[1] was done with more management and slight of art than the second. This, however, I will ever maintain, was not owing to any greater spirit of corruption; but only and solely to following the ancient dextrous ways, that had been, in a manner, engrained with the very nature of every thing pertaining to the representation of government as it existed, not merely in borough-towns, but wheresoever the crown and ministers found it expedient to have their lion's paw.

Matters were brought to a bearing differently, when, in the second edition of the late war,[2] it was thought necessary to call on the people to resist the rampageous ambition of Bonaparte, then champing and trampling for the rich pastures of our national commonwealth. Accordingly, I kept myself aloof from all handling in the pecuniaries of the business; but I lent a friendly countenance to every feasible project that was likely to strengthen the confidence of the king in the loyalty and bravery of his people. For by this time I had learnt, that there was a wake-rife[1] Common sense abroad among the opinions of men; and that the secret of the new way of ruling the world was to follow, not to control, the evident dictates of the popular voice; and I soon had reason to felicitate myself on this prudent and seasonable discovery. For it won me great reverence among the forward young men, who started up at the call of their country; and their demeanour towards me was as tokens and arles[2] from the rising generation, of being continued in respect and authority by them. Some of my colleagues, who are as well not named, by making themselves over busy, got but small thank for their pains. I was even pre-ferred to the Provost, as the medium of communicating the sentiments of the volunteering lads to the Lord-lieutenant;[3] and their cause did not suffer in my hands, for his Lordship had long been in the habit of considering me as one of the discreetest men in the borough; and although he returned very civil answers to all letters, he wrote to me in the cordial erudition of an old friend; a thing which the volunteers soon discerned, and respected me accordingly.

But the soldiering zeal being spontaneous among all ranks, and breaking forth into a blaze without any pre-ordered method, some of the magistrates were disconcerted, and wist not what to do. I'll no take it upon me to say, that they were altogether guided by a desire to have a finger in the pye, either in the shape of the honours of command, or the profits of contract; this, however, is certain, that they either felt or feigned a great alarm and consternation, at seeing such a vast military power in civil hands, over which they had no natural control; and, as was said, independent of the Crown and Parliament. Another thing there could be no doubt of: in the frame of this fear, they remonstrated with the government, and counselled the ministers to throw a wet blanket on the ardour of the volunteering; which, it is well known, was very readily done. For the ministers, on seeing such a pressing forward to join the banners of the kingdom, had a dread and regard to the old leaven of jacobinism, and put a limitation on the number of the armed men that were to be allowed to rise in every place; a most ill-advised prudence, as was made manifest by what happened among us; of which I will now rehearse the particulars, and the part I had in it myself.

As soon as it was understood among the commonality, that the French were determined to subdue and make a conquest of Britain, as they had done of all the rest of Europe, holding the noses of every continental king and potentate to the grindstone, there was a prodigious stir and motion in all the hearts and pulses of Scotland, and no where in a more vehement degree, than in Gudetown. But, for some reason or another, which I could never dive into the bottom of, there was a slackness or backwardness on the part of government in sending instructions to the magistrates to step forward; in so much, that the people grew terrified that they would be conquered, without having even an opportunity to defend, as their fathers did of old, the hallowed things of their native land; and, under the sense of this alarm, they knotted themselves together, and actually drew out proposals and resolutions of service of their own accord; by which means, they kept the power of choosing their officers in their own hands, and so gave many of the bigwigs of the town a tacit intimation, that they were not likely to have the command.

While things were in this process, the government had come to its senses; and some steps and measures were taken to organize volunteer corps throughout the nation. Taking heart from them, other corps were proposed on the part of the gentry, in which they were themselves to have the command; and seeing that the numbers were to be limited, they had a wish and interest to keep back the real volunteer offers, and to get their own accepted in their stead. A suspicion of this sort getting vent, an outcry of discontent thereat arose against them; and to the consternation of the magistrates, the young lads, who had at the first come so briskly forward, called a meeting of their body, and requesting the magistrates to be present, demanded to know what steps had been taken with their offer of service; and, if transmitted to government, what answer had been received.

This was a new era in public affairs; and no little amazement and anger was expressed by some of the town-council, that any set of persons should dare to question and interfere with the magistrates. But I saw it would never do to take the bull by the horns in that manner at such a time, so I commenced with Bailie Sprose, My Lord being at the time Provost, and earnestly beseeched him to attend the meeting with me, and to give a mild answer to any questions that might be put; and this was the more necessary, as there was some good reason to believe, that, in point of fact, the offer of service had been kept back.

We accordingly went to the meeting, where Mr. Sprose, at my suggestion, stated, that we had received no answer; and that we could not explain how the delay had arisen. This, however, did not pacify the volunteers; but they appointed certain of their own number, a committee, to attend to the business, and to communicate with the Secretary of State direct; intimating, that the members of the committee were those, whom they intended to elect for their officers. This was a decisive step, and took the business entirely out of the hands of the magistrates; so, after the meeting, both Mr. Sprose and myself agreed, that no time should be lost in communicating to the Lord-lieutenant what had taken place.

Our letter, and the volunteers' letter, went by the same post; and on receiving ours, the Lord-lieutenant had immediately some conference with the Secretary of State, who, falling into the views of his Lordship, in preferring the offers of the corps proposed by the gentry, sent the volunteers word in reply, that their services, on the terms they had proposed, which were of the least possible expence to government, could not be accepted.

It was hoped, that this answer would have ended the matter;

but there were certain propugnacious spirits in the volunteers' committee; and they urged and persuaded the others, to come into resolutions to the effect, that having made early offers of service, on terms less objectionable in every point than those of many offers subsequently made and accepted, unless their offer was accepted, they would consider themselves as having the authority of His Majesty's government to believe and to represent, that there was, in truth, no reason to apprehend that the enemy meditated any invasion; and these resolutions they sent off to London forthwith, before the magistrates had time to hear or to remonstrate against the use of such novel language from our borough to His Majesty's ministers.

We, however, heard something; and I wrote My Lord, to inform him, that the volunteers had renewed their offer, (for so we understood their representation was); and he, from what he had heard before from the Secretary of State, not expecting the effect it would have, answered me, that their offer could not be accepted. But, to our astonishment, by the same post, the volunteers found themselves accepted, and the gentlemen they recommended for their officers gazetted; the which, as I tell frankly, was an admonition to me, that the peremptory will of authority was no longer sufficient for the rule of mankind; and, therefore, I squared my after conduct more by a deference to public opinion, than by any laid down maxims and principles of my own. The consequence of which was, that my influence still continued to grow and gather strength in the community, and I was enabled to accomplish many things that my predecessors would have thought it was almost beyond the compass of man to undertake.

CHAPTER XXIX

CAPTAIN ARMOUR

In the course of these notandums, I have, here and there, touched on divers matters that did not actually pertain to my own magisterial life, further than as showing the temper and spirit in which different things were brought to a bearing; and, in the same way, I will now again step aside from the regular course of public affairs, to record an occurrence which, at the time, excited no small wonderment and sympathy, and in which it was confessed by many, that I performed a very judicious part. The event here spoken of, was the quartering in the town, after the removal of that well-behaved regiment, the Argyle fencibles, the main part of another, the name and number of which I do not now recollect; but it was an English corps, and, like the other troops of that nation, was not then brought into the sobriety of discipline to which the whole British army has since been reduced, by the paternal perseverance of His Royal Highness the Duke of York;[1] so that after the douce and respectful highlanders, we sorely felt the consequences of the outstropolous and galravitching[2] Englishers, who thought it no disgrace to fill themselves as fou[3] as pipers, and fight in the streets, and march to the church on the Lord's day, with their band of music. However, after the first Sunday, upon a remonstrance on the immorality of such irreligious bravery, Colonel Cavendish, the commandant, silenced the musicians.

Among the officers, there was one Captain Armour, an extraordinar well demeaned, handsome man, who was very shy of accepting any civility from the town gentry, and kept himself aloof from all our ploys and entertainments, in such a manner, that the rest of the officers talked of him, marvelling at the cause, for it was not his wont in other places.

One Sabbath, during the remembering prayer, Mr. Pittle put up a few words for criminals under sentence of death, there being two at the time in the Ayr jail, at the which petition, I happened to look at Captain Armour, who, with the lave[1] of the officers, were within the magistrate's loft, and I thought he·had, at the moment, a likeness to poor Jeanie Gaisling, that was executed for the murder of her bastard bairn.

This notion at the time disturbed me very much, and one thought after another so came into my head, that I could pay no attention to Mr. Pittle, who certainly was but a cauldrife[2] preacher, and never more so than on that day. In short, I was haunted with the fancy, that Captain Armour was no other than the misfortunate lassie's poor brother, who had in so pathetical a manner, attended her and the magistrates to the scaffold; and what was very strange, I was not the only one in the kirk who thought the same thing; for the resemblance, while Mr. Pittle was praying, had been observed by many, and it was the subject of discourse in my shop on the Monday following, when the whole history of that most sorrowful concern was again brought to mind. But, without dwelling at large on the particularities, I need only mention, that it began to be publicly jealoused,[3] that he was indeed the identical lad, which moved every body; for he was a very good and gallant officer, having risen by his own merits, and was likewise much beloved in the regiment. Nevertheless, though his sister's sin was no fault of his, and could not impair the worth of his well-earned character, yet some of the thoughtless young ensigns began to draw off from him, and he was visited, in a manner, with the disgrace of an excommunication.

Being, however, a sensible man, he bore it for a while patiently, may be hoping that the suspicion would wear away; but My Lord, with all his retinue, coming from London to the castle for the summer, invited the officers one day to dine with him and the Countess, when the fact was established by a very simple accident.

Captain Armour, in going up the stairs, and along the crooked old passages of the castle, happened to notice that the Colonel, who was in the van, turned to the wrong hand, and called to him to take the other way, which circumstance convinced all present that he was domestically familiar with the labyrinths of the building; and the consequence was, that, during dinner, not one of the officers spoke to him, some from embarrassment, and others from pride.

The Earl perceiving their demeanour, enquired of the Colonel, when they had returned from the table to the drawing-room, as to the cause of such a visible alienation, and Colonel Cavendish, who was much of the gentleman, explaining it, expressing his grief that so unpleasant a discovery had been made to the prejudice of so worthy a man, My Lord was observed to stand some time in a thoughtful posture, after which he went and spoke in a whisper to the Countess, who advised him, as her ladyship in the sequel told me herself, to send for me, as a wary and prudent man. Accordingly a servant was secretly despatched express to the town on that errand; My Lord and My Lady insisting on the officers staying to spend the evening with them, which was an unusual civility at the *pro forma* dinners at the castle.

When I arrived, the Earl took me into his private library, and we had some serious conversation about the Captain's sister; and when I had related the circumstantialities of her end to him, he sent for the Captain, and with great tenderness, and a manner most kind and gracious, told him what he had noticed in the conduct of the officers, offering his mediation to appease any difference, if it was a thing that could be done.

While My Lord was speaking, the Captain perserved a steady and unmoved countenance; no one could have imagined that he was listening to any thing, but some grave generality of discourse; but when the Earl offered to mediate, his breast swelled, and his face grew like his coat, and I saw his eyes fill with water as he turned round, to hide the grief that could not be stifled. The passion of shame, however, lasted but for a moment. In less time than I am in writing these heads, he was again himself, and with a modest fortitude that was exceedingly comely, he acknowledged who he was, adding, that he feared his blameless disgrace entailed effects which he could not hope to remove, and therefore it was his intention to resign his commission. The Earl, however, requested that he would do nothing rashly, and that he should first allow him to try what could be done to convince his brother officers, that it was unworthy of them to act towards him in the way they did. His Lordship then led us to the drawing-room, on entering which, he said aloud to the Countess, in a manner that could not be misunderstood, 'In Captain Armour I have discovered an old acquaintance, who, by his own merits, and under circumstances that would have sunk any man less conscious of his own purity and worth, has raised himself, from having once been my servant, to a rank that makes me happy to receive him as my guest.'

I need not add, that this benevolence of his Lordship was followed with a most bountiful alteration towards the Captain from all present, in so much, that before the regiment was removed from the town, we had the satisfaction of seeing him at divers of the town-ploys, where he received every civility.

CHAPTER XXX

THE TRADES' BALL

AT the conclusion of my second Provostry,[1] or rather, as I think, after it was over, an accident happened in the town that might have led to no little trouble and contention, but for the way and manner that I managed the same. My friend and neighbour, Mr. Kilsyth, an ettling[2] man, who had been wonderful prosperous in the spirit line, having been taken on for a bailie, by virtue of some able handling, on the part of

Deacon Kenitweel, proposed and propounded, that there should be a ball and supper for the trades; and to testify his sense of the honour that he owed to all the crafts, especially the wrights, whereof Mr. Kenitweel was then deacon, he promised to send in both wine, rum, and brandy, from his cellar, for the company. I did not much approve of the project, for divers reasons; the principal of which was, because my daughters were grown into young ladies, and I was, thank God, in a circumstance to entitle them to hold their heads something above the trades. However, I could not positively refuse my compliance, especially as Mrs. Pawkie was requested by Bailie Kilsyth, and those who took an active part in furtherance of the ploy, to be the lady directress of the occasion. And, out of an honour and homage to myself, I was likewise entreated to preside at the head of the table, over the supper that was to ensue after the dancing.

In its own nature, there was surely nothing of an objectionable principle, in a 'trades' ball;' but we had several young men of the gentle sort about the town, blythe and rattling lads, who were welcome both to high and low, and to whom the project seemed worthy of a ridicule. It would, as I said at the time, have been just as well to have made it really a trades' ball, without any adulteration of the gentry; but the hempies alluded to jouked themselves[1] in upon us, and obligated the managers to invite them; and an ill return they made for this discretion and civility, as I have to relate.

On the night set for the occasion, the company met in the assembly-room, in the New-inns, where we had bespoke a light genteel supper, and had M'Lachlan, the fiddler, over from Ayr, for the purpose. Nothing could do better, while the dancing lasted; the whole concern wore an appearance of the greatest genteelity. But when supper was announced, and the company adjourned to partake of it, judge of the universal consternation that was visible in every countenance, when, instead of the light tarts, and nice jellies and sillybobs[2]

that were expected, we beheld a long table, with a row down
the middle of rounds of beef, large cold veal-pyes on pewter
plates, like tea-trays, cold boiled turkies, and beef and bacon
hams, and, for ornament in the middle, a perfect stack of
cellary.

The instant I entered the supper-room, I saw there had
been a plot; poor Bailie Kilsyth, who had all the night been in
triumph and glory, was for a season speechless; and when at
last he came to himself, he was like to have been the death of
the landlord on the spot, while I could remark, with the tail of
my eye, that secret looks of a queer satisfaction were
exchanged among the beaux before mentioned. This observe,
when I made it, led me to go up to the bailie, as he was
storming at the bribed and corrupt inn-keeper, and to say to
him, that if he would leave the matter to me, I would settle it
to the content of all present; which he, slackening the grip he
had taken of the landlord by the throat, instantly conceded.
Whereupon, I went back to the head of the table, and said
aloud, 'that the cold collection had been provided by some
secret friends, and although it was not just what the directors
could have wished, yet it would be as well to bring to mind
the old proverb, which instructs us no to be particular about
the mouth of a gi'en horse.'[1] But I added, 'before partaking
thereof, we'll hae in our bill frae the landlord, and settle it,'—
and it was called accordingly. I could discern, that this was a
turn that the conspirators did not look for. It, however, put
the company a thought into spirits, and they made the best
o't. But while they were busy at the table, I took a canny
opportunity of saying, under the rose to one of the gentlemen, 'that I saw through the joke, and could relish it just as
well as the plotters; but as the thing was so plainly felt as an
insult by the generality of the company, the less that was said
about it the better; and that if the whole bill, including the
cost of Bailie Kilsyth's wine and spirits, was defrayed, I would
make no enquiries, and the authors might never be known.
This admonishment was not lost, for by and bye, I saw the

gentlemen confabbing together; and the next morning, through the post, I received a twenty-pound note, in a nameless letter, requesting the amount of it to be placed against the expence of the ball. I was overly well satisfied with this, to say a great deal of what I thought, but I took a quiet step to the bank, where, expressing some doubt of the goodness of the note, I was informed it was perfectly good, and had been that very day issued from the bank to one of the gentlemen, whom, even at this day, it would not be prudent to expose to danger by naming.

Upon a consultation with the other gentlemen, who had the management of the ball, it was agreed, that we should say nothing of the gift of twenty pounds, but distribute it in the winter to needful families, which was done; for we feared that the authors of the derision would be found out, and that ill-blood might be bred in the town.

CHAPTER XXXI

THE BAILIE'S HEAD

BUT although in the main I was considered by the events and transactions already rehearsed, a prudent and sagacious man, yet I was not free from the consequences of envy. To be sure, they were not manifested in any very intolerant spirit, and in so far they caused me rather molestation of mind than actual suffering; but still they kithed in evil,[1] and thereby marred the full satisfactory fruition of my labours and devices. Among other of the outbreakings alluded to that not a little vexed me, was one that I will relate, and just in order here to show the animus of men's minds towards me.

We had in the town a clever lad, with a geni of a mechanical turn, who made punch-bowls of leather, and legs for cripples of the same commodity, that were lighter and easier to wear than either legs of cork or timber. His name was Geordie Sooplejoint, a modest, douce, and well-behaved young man—caring for little else but the perfecting of his art. I had heard of his talent, and was curious to converse with him; so I spoke to Bailie Pirlet, who had taken him by the hand, to bring him and his leather punch-bowl, and some of his curious legs and arms, to let me see them; the which the Bailie did, and it happened that while they were with me, in came Mr. Thomas M'Queerie, a dry neighbour at a joke.

After some generality of discourse concerning the inventions, whereon Bailie Pirlet, who was naturally a gabby prick-me-dainty bodie,[1] enlarged at great length, with all his well dockit[2] words, as if they were on chandler's pins,[3] pointing out here the utility of the legs to persons maimed in the wars of their country, and showing forth there, in what manner the punch-bowls were specimens of a new art that might in time supplant both China and Staffordshire ware, and deducing there-from the benefits that would come out of it to the country at large, and especially to the landed interest, in so much as the increased demand which it would cause for leather, would raise the value of hides, and per consequence the price of black cattle—to all which, Mr. M'Queerie listened with a shrewd and a thirsty ear; and when the bailie had made an end of his pater-noster, he proposed that I should make a filling of Geordie's bowl, to try if it did not leak.

'Indeed, Mr. Pawkie,' quo' he, 'it will be a great credit to our town to hae had the merit o' producing sic a clever lad, who, as the bailie has in a manner demonstrated, is ordained to bring about an augmentation o' trade by his punch-bowls, little short of what has been done wi' the steam engines. Geordie will be to us what James Watt is to the ettling[4] town of Greenock, so we can do no less than drink prosperity to his endeavours.'

I did not much like this bantering of Mr. M'Queerie, for I saw it made Geordie's face grow red, and it was not what he had deserved; so to repress it, and to encourage the poor lad, I said, 'Come, come, neighbour, none of your wipes[1]—what Geordie has done, is but arles[2] of what he may do.'

'That's not to be debated,' replied Mr. M'Queerie, 'for he has shown already that he can make very good legs and arms; and I'm sure I should na be surprised were he in time to make heads as good as a bailie's.'

I never saw any mortal man look as that pernicketty personage, the bailie, did at this joke, but I suppressed my own feelings; while the bailie, like a bantam cock in a passion, stotted out of his chair with the spunk of a birslet pea,[3] demanding of Mr. M'Queerie an explanation of what he meant by the insinuation. It was with great difficulty that I got him pacified; but unfortunately the joke was oure[4] good to be forgotten, and when it was afterwards spread abroad, as it happened to take its birth in my house, it was laid to my charge, and many a time was I obligated to tell all about it, and how it could na be meant for me, but had been incurred by Bailie Pirlet's conceit of spinning out long prejinck[5] speeches.

CHAPTER XXXII

THE TOWN DRUMMER

NOR did I get every thing my own way, for I was often thwarted in matters of small account, and suffered from them greater disturbance and molestation than things of such little moment ought to have been allowed to produce within me; and I do not think that any thing happened in the whole course of my public life, which gave me more vexation than what I felt in the last week of my second provostry.

For many a year, one Robin Boss had been town drummer; he was a relic of some American-war fencibles, and was, to say the God's truth of him, a divor bodie,[6] with no manner of

conduct, saving a very earnest endeavour to fill himself fou
as often as he could get the means; the consequence of which
was, that his face was as plooky as a curran bun,[1] and his nose
as red as a partan's tae.[2]

One afternoon there was a need to send out a proclamation
to abolish a practice that was growing into a custom, in some
of the bye parts of the town, of keeping swine at large—
ordering them to be confined in proper styes, and other
suitable places.—As on all occasions when the matter to be
proclaimed was from the magistrates, Thomas, on this, was
attended by the town-officers in their Sunday garbs, and with
their halberts in their hands; but the abominable and
irreverent creature was so drunk, that he wamblet[3] to and fro
over the drum, as if there had not been a bane in his body. He
was seemingly as soople and as senseless as a bolster.—Still,
as this was no new thing with him, it might have passed; for
James Hound, the senior officer, was in the practice, when
Robin was in that state, of reading the proclamations himself.
—On this occasion, however, James happened to be absent
on some hue and cry quest, and another of the officers (I
forget which,) was appointed to perform for him. Robin,
accustomed to James, no sooner heard the other man begin to
read, than he began to curse and swear at him as an incapable
nincompoop—an impertinent term that he was much
addicted to. The grammar school was at the time skayling,[4]
and the boys seeing the stramash,[5] gathered round the officer,
and yelling and shouting, encouraged Robin more and more
into rebellion, till at last they worked up his corruption[6] to
such a pitch, that he took the drum from about his neck, and
made it fly like a bomb-shell at the officer's head.

The officers behaved very well, for they dragged Robin by
the lug and the horn to the tolbooth, and then came with their
complaint to me. Seeing how the authorities had been set at
nought, and the necessity there was of making an example, I
forthwith ordered Robin to be cashiered from the service of
the town, and as so important a concern as a proclamation

ought not to be delayed, I likewise, upon the spot, ordered the officers to take a lad that had been also a drummer in a marching regiment, and go with him to make the proclamation.

Nothing could be done in a more earnest and zealous public spirit than this was done by me.—But habit had begot in the town a partiality for the drunken, neer-do-well Robin, and this just act of mine was immediately condemned as a daring stretch of arbitrary power; and the consequence was, that when the council met next day, some sharp words flew among us, as to my usurping an undue authority, and the thank I got for my pains was the mortification to see the worthless body restored to full power and dignity, with no other reward than an admonition to behave better for the future. Now, I leave it to the unbiassed judgment of posterity to determine if any public man could be more ungraciously treated by his colleagues than I was on this occasion.—But, verily, the council had their reward.

CHAPTER XXXIII

AN ALARM

THE divor, Robin Boss, being, as I have recorded, reinstated in office, soon began to play his old tricks.—In the course of the week after the Michaelmas term at which my second provostry ended, he was so insupportably drunk, that he fell head foremost into his drum, which cost the town five-and-twenty shillings for a new one,[1]—an accident that was not without some satisfaction to me, and I trow I was not sparing in my derisive commendations on the worth of such a public officer;—nevertheless he was still kept on, some befriending him for compassion, and others as it were to spite me.

But Robin's good behaviour did not end with breaking the

drum, and costing a new one.—In the course of the winter it was his custom to beat, 'Go to bed, Tom,' about ten o'clock at night, and the reveillè at five in the morning.—In one of his drunken fits he made a mistake, and instead of going his rounds as usual at ten o'clock, he had fallen asleep in a change house,[1] and waking about the midnight hour in the terror of some whisky dream, he seized his drum, and running into the streets, began to strike the fire-beat[2] in the most awful manner.

It was a fine clear frosty moonlight, and the hollow sound of the drum resounded through the silent streets like thunder.—In a moment every body was a foot, and the cry of 'Whar is't? whar's the fire?' was heard echoing from all sides.—Robin, quite unconscious that he alone was the cause of the alarm, still went along beating the dreadful summons. I heard the noise and rose, but while I was drawing on my stockings, in the chair at the bed head, and telling Mrs. Pawkie to compose herself, for our houses were all insured,[3] I suddenly recollected that Robin had the night before neglected to go his rounds at ten o'clock as usual, and the thought came into my head that the alarm might be one of his inebriated mistakes; so instead of dressing myself any farther, I went to the window, and looked out through the glass, without opening it, for, being in my night clothes, I was afraid of taking cold.

The street was as throng[4] as on a market day, and every face in the moonlight was pale with fear.—Men and lads were running with their coats, and carrying their breeches in their hands; wives and maidens were all asking questions at one another, and even lasses were fleeing to and fro, like water nymphs with urns, having stoups and pails in their hands.—There was swearing and tearing of men, hoarse with the rage of impatience, at the Tolbooth, getting out the fire engine from its stance under the stair; and loud and terrible afar off, and over all, came the peal of alarm from drunken Robin's drum.

I could scarcely keep my composity when I beheld and heard all this, for I was soon thoroughly persuaded of the

fact. At last I saw Deacon Girdwood, the chief advocate and
champion of Robin, passing down the causey like a demented
man, with a red night-cap, and his big coat on—for some had
cried[1] that the fire was in his yard.—'Deacon,' cried I,
opening the window, forgetting in the jocularity of the
moment the risk I ran from being so naked; 'whar away sae
fast, Deacon?'

The Deacon stopped and said, 'Is't out? is't out?'

'Gang your ways home,' quo' I very coolly, 'for I hae a
notion that a' this hobbleshaw's[2] but the fume of a gill in your
friend Robin's head.'

'It's no possible,' exclaimed the Deacon.

'Possible here or possible there, Mr. Girdwood,' quo' I,
'it's oure cauld[3] for me to stand talking wi' you here; we'll
learn the rights o't in the morning; so, good night;' and with
that I pulled down the window. But scarcely had I done so,
when a shout of laughter came gathering up the street, and
soon after poor drunken Robin was brought along by the cuff
of the neck, between two of the town-officers, one of them
carrying his drum. The next day he was put out of office for
ever, and folk recollecting in what manner I had acted
towards him before, the outcry about my arbitrary power was
forgotten in the blame that was heaped upon those who had
espoused Robin's cause against me.

CHAPTER XXXIV

THE COUNTRY GENTRY

FOR a long period of time, I had observed that there was a
gradual mixing in of the country gentry among the town's
folks. This was partly to be ascribed to a necessity rising out of
the French Revolution, whereby men of substance thought it
an expedient policy to relax in their ancient maxims of family

pride and consequence; and partly to the great increase and growth of wealth which the influx of trade caused throughout the kingdom, whereby the merchants were enabled to vie and ostentate even with the better sort of lairds. The effect of this, however, was less protuberant in our town than in many others which I might well name, and the cause thereof lay mainly in our being more given to deal in the small way; not that we lacked of traders possessed both of purse and perseverance; but we did not exactly lie in the thoroughfare of those mighty masses of foreign commodities, the through-going of which left, to use the words of the old proverb, 'goud in goupins,'[1] with all who had the handling of the same. Nevertheless, we came in for our share of the condescensions of the country gentry; and although there was nothing like a melting down of them among us, either by marrying or giving in marriage, there was a communion that gave us some insight, no overly to their advantage, as to the extent and measure of their capacities and talents. In short, we discovered that they were vessels made of ordinary human clay; so that, instead of our reverence for them being augmented by a freer intercourse, we thought less and less of them, until, poor bodies, the bit prideful lairdies were just looked down upon by our gausie[2] big-bellied burgesses, not a few of whom had heritable bonds on their estates. But in this I am speaking of the change when it had come to a full head; for in verity it must be allowed, that when the country gentry, with their families, began to intromit[3] among us, we could not make enough of them. Indeed, we were deaved about the affability of old crabbit Bodle,[4] of Bodletonbrae, and his sister, Miss Jenny, when they favoured us with their company at the first inspection ball. I'll ne'er forget that occasion; for being then in my second provostry, I had, in course of nature, been appointed a deputy Lord-lieutenant, and the town-council entertaining the inspecting officers, and the officers of the volunteers, it fell as a duty incumbent on me to be the director of the ball afterwards, and to the which I sent an invitation to the laird and his sister, little hoping or expecting they would come. But the laird, likewise being a deputy Lord-lieutenant, he accepted the invitation, and came with his sister in all the state of pedigree in their power. Such a prodigy of old-fashioned grandeur as Miss Jenny was—but neither shop nor mantua-maker of our day and generation had been the better o't. She was just, as some of the young lasses said, like Clarissa Harlowe, in the cuts and copper-plates[1] of Mrs. Rickerton's set of the book, and an older and more curious set than Mrs. Rickerton's was not in the whole town; indeed, for that matter, I believe it was the only one among us, and it had edified, as Mr. Binder the bookseller used to say, at least three successive generations of young ladies, for he had himself given it twice new covers. We had, however, not then any circulating library. But for all her antiquity and lappets,[2] it is not be supposed what respect and deference Miss Jenny and her brother, the laird, received —nor the small praise that came to my share, for having had the spirit to invite them. The ball was spoken of as the genteelest in the memory of man, although, to my certain knowledge, on account of the volunteers, some were there that never thought to mess or mell in the same chamber with Bodletonbrae and his sister, Miss Jenny.

CHAPTER XXXV

TESTS OF SUCCESS

INTENDING these notations for the instruction of posterity, it would not be altogether becoming of me to speak of the domestic effects which many of the things that I have herein jotted down had in my own family. I feel myself, however, constrained in spirit to lift aside a small bit of the private curtain, just to show how Mrs. Pawkie comported herself in the progressive vicissitudes of our prosperity, in the act and doing of which I do not wish to throw any slight on her feminine qualities, for, to speak of her as she deserves at my hand, she has been a most excellent wife, and a decent woman, and had aye a ruth[1] and ready hand for the needful. Still, to say the truth, she is not without a few little weaknesses like her neighbours, and the ill-less vanity of being thought far ben[2] with the great is among others of her harmless frailties.

Soon after the inspection ball before spoken of, she said to me that it would be a great benefit and advantage to our family if we could get Bodletonbrae and his sister, and some of the other country gentry, to dine with us. I was not very clear about how the benefit was to come to book, for the outlay I thought as likely to o'ergang the profit; at the same time, not wishing to balk Mrs. Pawkie of a ploy on which I saw her mind was bent, I gave my consent to her and my daughters to send out the cards, and make the necessary preparations. But herein I should not take credit to myself for more of the virtue of humility than was my due; therefore I open the door of my secret heart so far ajee,[3] as to let the reader discern that I was content to hear our invitations were all accepted.

Of the specialities and dainties of the banquet prepared, it is not fitting that I should treat in any more particular manner, than to say they were the best that could be had, and that our guests were all mightily well pleased. Indeed, my wife was out of the body with exultation, when Mrs. Auchans of that Ilk, begged that she would let her have a copy of the directions she had followed in making a flummery, which the whole company declared was most excellent.—This compliment was the more pleasant, as Lady Auchans was well known for her skill in savoury contrivances, and to have any thing new to her of the sort, was a triumph beyond our most sanguine expectations. In a word, from that day we found that we had taken, as it were, a step above the common in the town; there were, no doubt, some who envied our good fortune; but, upon the whole, the community at large were pleased to see the consideration in which their chief magistrate was held. It reflected down, as it were, upon themselves, a glaik[1] of the sunshine that shone upon us; and, although it may be a light thing, as it is seemingly a vain one, to me to say, I am now pretty much of Mrs. Pawkie's opinion, that our cultivation of an intercourse with the country gentry was, in the end, a benefit to our family, in so far as it obtained, both for my sons and daughters, a degree of countenance that otherwise could hardly have been expected from their connections and fortune, even though I had been twice provost.

CHAPTER XXXVI

RETRIBUTION

BUT a sad accident shortly after happened, which had the effect of making it as little pleasant to me to vex Mr. Hickery with a joke about the Tappit-hen, as it was to him. Widow Fenton, as I have soberly hinted, for it is not a subject to be openly spoken of, had many ill-assorted and irregular characters among her customers, and a gang of play-actors coming to the town, and getting leave to perform in Mr. Dribble's barn, batches of the young lads, both gentle and semple, when the play was over, used to adjourn to her house for pyes and porter, the commodities in which she chiefly dealt. One night, when the deep tragedy of Mary Queen of Scots was the play, there was a great concourse of people, at 'The Theatre Royal,'[2] and the consequence was, that the Tappit-hen's house, both but and ben, was, at the conclusion, filled to overflowing.

The actress that played Queen Elizabeth, was a little-worth termagant woman, and, in addition to other laxities of conduct, was addicted to the immorality of taking more than

did her good, and when in her cups, she would rant and ring¹
fiercer than old Queen Elizabeth ever could do herself. Queen
Mary's part was done by a bonny genty young lady, that was
said to have run away from a boarding school, and, by all
accounts, she acted wonderful well. But she too was not
altogether without a flaw, so that there was a division in the
town between their admirers and visitors, some maintaining,
as I was told, that Mrs. Beaufort, if she would keep herself
sober, was not only a finer woman, but more of a lady, and a
better actress, than Miss Scarborough, while others considered her as a vulgar regimental virago.

   The play of Mary Queen of Scots, causing a great congregation of the rival partizans of the two ladies to meet in the
Tappit-hen's publick, some contention took place about the
merits of their respective favourites, and, from less to more,
hands were raised, and blows given, and the trades-lads, being
as hot in their differences as the gentlemen, a dreadful riot
ensued. Gill-stoups, porter bottles, and penny pyes flew like
balls and bomb-shells in battle. Mrs. Fenton, with her mutch
off, and her hair loose, with wide and wild arms, like a witch
in a whirlwind, was seen trying to sunder the challengers,
and the champions. Finding however her endeavours un-
availing, and fearing that murder would be committed, she
ran like desperation into the streets, crying for help. I was just
at the time stepping into my bed, when I heard the uproar,
and dressing myself again, I went out to the street; for the
sound and din of the riot came raging through the silence of
the midnight, like the tearing and swearing of the multitude
at a house on fire, and I thought no less an accident could be
the cause.

   On going into the street, I met several persons running to
the scene of action, and, among others, Mrs. Beaufort, with a
gallant of her own, and both of them no in their sober senses.
It's no for me to say who he was, but assuredly had the
woman no been doited² with drink, she never would have
seen any likeness between him and me, for he was more than

twenty years my junior. However, onward we all ran to Mrs.
Fenton's house, where the riot, like a raging cauldron boiling
o'er, had overflowed into the street.

The moment I reached the door, I ran forward with my
stick raised, but not with any design of striking man, woman,
or child, when a ramplor[1] devil, the young laird of Swinton,
who was one of the most outstrapolous rakes about the town,
wrenched it out of my grip, and would have, I dare say, made
no scruple of doing me some dreadful bodily harm, when
suddenly I found myself pulled out of the crowd by a powerful
handed woman, who cried, 'Come, my love; love, come:' and
who was this, but that scarlet strumpet, Mrs. Beaufort, who
having lost her gallant in the crowd, and being, as I think,
blind fou, had taken me for him, insisting before all present,
that I was her dear friend, and that she would die for me,—
with other siclike fantastical and randy[2] ranting, which no
queen in a tragedy could by any possibility surpass.—At first
I was confounded, and overtaken, and could not speak; and
the worst of all was, that, in a moment, the mob seemed to
forget their quarrel, and to turn in derision on me. What
might have ensued it would not be easy to say, but just at this
very critical juncture, and while the drunken latheron[3] was
casting herself into antic shapes of distress, and flourishing
with her hands and arms to the heavens at my imputed
cruelty, two of the town-officers came up, which gave me
courage to act a decisive part, so I gave over to them Mrs.
Beaufort, with all her airs, and going myself to the guard-
house, brought a file of soldiers, and so quelled the riot. But
from that night I thought it prudent to eschew every
allusion to Mrs. Fenton, and tacitly to forgive even Swinton
for the treatment I had received from him, by seeming as if I
had not noticed him, although I had singled him out by name.

Mrs. Pawkie, on hearing what I had suffered from Mrs.
Beaufort, was very zealous that I should punish her to the
utmost rigour of the law, even to drumming her out of the
town; but forbearance was my best policy, so I only

persuaded my colleagues to order the players to decamp,[1] and to give the Tappit-hen notice, that it would be expedient for the future sale of her pyes and porter, at untimeous hours, that she should flit her howff[2] from our town. Indeed, what pleasure would it have been to me to have dealt unmercifully, either towards the one or the other? for surely the gentle way of keeping up a proper respect for magistrates, and others in authority, should ever be preferred; especially, as in cases like this, where there had been no premeditated wrong. And I say this with the greater sincerity, for in my secret conscience, when I think of the affair at this distance of time, I am pricked not a little in reflecting how I had previously crowed and triumphed over poor Mr. Hickery, in the matter of his mortification at the time of Miss Peggy Dainty's false step.

CHAPTER XXXVII

THE DUEL

HERETOFORE all my magisterial undertakings and concerns had thriven in a very satisfactory manner. I was to be sure, now and then, as I have narrated, subjected to opposition, and squibs, and a jeer; and envious and spiteful persons were not wanting in the world to call in question my intents and motives, representing my best endeavours for the public good as but a right-handed method to secure my own interests. It would be a vain thing of me to deny, that, at the beginning of my career, I was misled by the wily examples of the past times, who thought that in taking on them to serve the community, they had a privilege to see that they were full handed for what benefit they might do the public; but as I gathered experience, and saw the rising of the sharp-sighted spirit that is now abroad among the affairs of men, I clearly discerned, that it would be more for the advantage of me and mine to act with a conformity thereto, than to seek, by any similar wiles or devices, an immediate and sicker advantage.— I may, therefore, say, without a boast, that the two or three years before my third provostry were as renowned and comfortable to myself, upon the whole, as any reasonable man could look for. We cannot, however, expect a full cup and measure of the sweets of life, without some adulteration of the sour and bitter, and it was my lot and fate to prove an experience of this truth, in a sudden and unaccountable falling off from all moral decorum in the person of my brother's only son, Richard, a lad that was a promise of great ability in his youth.

He was just between the tyning and the winning,[1] as the saying is, when the play-actors, before spoken of, came to the town, being then in his eighteenth year. Naturally of a light-hearted and funny[2] disposition, and possessing a jocose turn for mimickry, he was a great favourite among his companions, and getting in with the players, it seems drew up with that little-worth, demure daffodel, Miss Scarborough, through the instrumentality of whose condisciples and the randy Mrs. Beaufort, that riot at widow Fenton's began, which ended in expurgating the town of the whole gang, bag and baggage. Some there were, I shall here mention, who said that the expulsion of the players was owing to what I had heard anent the intromission of my nephew; but, in verity, I had not the least spunk,[3] or spark of suspicion, of what was going on between him and the Miss, till one night, some time after, Richard, and the young laird of Swinton, with others of their comrades, forgathered, and came to high words on the subject, the two being rivals, or rather, as was said, equally in esteem and favour with the lady.

Young Swinton was, to say the truth of him, a fine bold rattling lad, warm in the temper, and ready with the hand, and no man's foe so much as his own; for he was a spoiled bairn, through the partiality of old Lady Bodikins, his grand-

mother, who lived in the turretted house at the town-end, by
whose indulgence he grew to be of a dressy and rakish
inclination, and, like most youngsters of the kind, was vain of
his shames, the which cost Mr. Pittle's session no little
trouble. But, not to dwell on his faults—my nephew and he
quarrelled, and nothing less would serve them than to fight a
duel; which they did with pistols next morning, and Richard
received from the laird's first shot a bullet in the left arm, that
disabled him in that member for life. He was left for dead on
the Green where they fought—Swinton and the two seconds
making, as was supposed, their escape.

When Richard was found faint and bleeding, by Tammy
Tout, the town-herd, as he drove out the cows in the morning,
the hobbleshow[1] is not to be described, and my brother came
to me, and insisted that I should give him a warrant to
apprehend all concerned. I was grieved for my brother, and
very much distressed to think of what had happened to blithe
Dicky, as I was wont to call my nephew when he was a laddie,
and I would fain have gratified the spirit of revenge in myself.
But I brought to mind his roving and wanton pranks, and I
counselled his father first to abide the upshot of the wound,
representing to him, in the best manner I could, that it was
but the quarrel of young men, and that may be his son was as
muckle in fault as Swinton.

My brother was, however, of a hasty temper, and upbraided
me with my slackness, on account, as he tauntingly insinuated,
of the young laird being one of my best customers, which
was a harsh and unrighteous doing; but it was not the severest
trial which the accident occasioned to me.—For the same
night, at a late hour, a line was brought to me by a lassie,
requesting I would come to a certain place, and when I went
there, who was it from but Swinton and the two other young
lads that had been the seconds at the duel.

'Bailie,' said the laird on behalf of himself and friends,
'though you are the uncle of poor Dick, we have resolved to
throw ourselves into your hands, for we have not provided

any money to enable us to flee the country; we only hope you will not deal overly harshly with us, till his fate is ascertained.'

I was greatly disconcerted, and wist not what to say; for knowing the rigour of our Scottish laws against duelling, I was wae to see three brave youths not yet come to years of discretion, standing in the peril and jeopardy of an ignominious end,[1] and that too for an injury done to my own kin; and then I thought of my nephew, and of my brother, that, may be, would soon be in sorrow for the loss of his only son. In short, I was tried almost beyond my humanity. The three poor lads seeing me hesitate, were much moved, and one of them (Sandy Blackie) said, 'I told you how it would be; it was even down madness to throw ourselves into the lion's mouth.' To this Swinton replied, 'Mr. Pawkie, we have cast ourselves on your mercy as a gentleman.'

What could I say to this, but that I hoped they would find me one, and without speaking any more at that time, for indeed I could not, my heart beat so fast, I bade them follow me, and taking them round by the back road to my garden yett,[2] I let them in, and conveyed them into a warehouse where I kept my bales and boxes. Then slipping into the house, I took out of the pantry a basket of bread and a cold leg of mutton, which, when Mrs. Pawkie and the servant lassies missed in the morning, they could not divine what had become of, and giving the same to them, with a bottle of wine, for they were very hungry, having tasted nothing all day, I went round to my brother's, to see at the latest how Richard was.—But such a stang[3] as I got on entering the house, when I heard his mother wailing that he was dead, he having fainted away in getting the bullet extracted; and when I saw his father coming out of the room like a demented man, and heard again his upbraiding of me for having refused a warrant to apprehend the murderers, I was so stunned with the shock, and with the thought of the poor young lads in my mercy, that I could with difficulty support myself along the passage into a room where there was a chair, into which I fell rather than threw myself. I had not, however, been long seated, when a joyful cry announced that Richard was recovering, and presently he was in a manner free from pain, and the doctor assured me the wound was probably not mortal. I did not, however, linger long on hearing this, but hastening home, I took what money I had in my scrutoire, and going to the malefactors, said, 'Lads, take thir twa three pounds,[1] and quit the town as fast as ye can, for Richard is my nephew, and blood, ye ken, is thicker than water, and I may be tempted to give you up.'

They started on their legs, and shaking me in a warm manner by both the hands, they hurried away without speaking, nor could I say more, as I opened the back yett to let them out, than bid them take tent of themselves.

Mrs. Pawkie was in a great consternation at my late absence, and when I went home she thought I was ill, I was so pale and flurried, and she wanted to send for the doctor, but I told her that when I was calmed, I would be better; however, I got no sleep that night. In the morning I went to see Richard, whom I found in a composed and rational state; he confessed to his father that he was as muckle to blame as Swinton, and begged and entreated us, if he should die, not to take any steps against the fugitives; my brother, however, was loth to make rash promises, and it was not till his son was out of danger that I had any ease of mind for the part I had played. But when Richard was afterwards well enough to go about, and the duellers had came out of their hidings, they told him what I had done, by which the whole affair came to the public, and I got great fame thereby, none being more proud to speak of it than poor Dick himself, who, from that time, became the bosom friend of Swinton; in so much, that when he was out of his time, as a writer,[2] and had gone through his courses at Edinburgh, the laird made him his man of business, and, in a manner, gave him a nest egg.

CHAPTER XXXVIII

AN INTERLOCUTOR [1]

UPON a consideration of many things, it appears to me very strange, that almost the whole tot of our improvements became, in a manner, the parents of new plagues and troubles to the Magistrates. It might reasonably have been thought that the lamps in the streets would have been a terror to evil-doers, and the plain-stone side-pavements paths of pleasant-ness to them that do well; but so far from this being the case, the very reverse was the consequence. The servant lasses went freely out (on their errands) at night, and at late hours, for their mistresses, without the protection of lanthorns, by which they were enabled to gallant in a way that never could have before happened: for lanthorns are kent-speckle [2] commodities, and of course a check on every kind of gavaulling. [3] Thus, out of the lamps sprung no little irregu-larity in the conduct of servants, and much bitterness of spirit on that account to mistresses, especially to those who were of a particular turn, and who did not choose that their maidens should spend their hours a field, when they could be profitably employed at home.

Of the plagues that were from the plain-stones, I have given an exemplary specimen in the plea between old prejink [4] Miss Peggy Dainty, and the widow Fenton, that was commonly called the Tappit-hen. For the present, I shall therefore confine myself in this *nota bene* to an accident that happened to Mrs. Girdwood, the deacon of the coopers wife—a most managing, industrious, and indefatigable woman, that allowed no grass to grow in her path.

Mrs. Girdwood had feed one Jeanie Tirlet, and soon after she came home, the mistress had her big summer washing at the public washing-house on the Green [5]—all the best of her sheets and napery—both what had been used in the course of the winter, and what was only washed to keep clear in the colour, were in the boyne.[1] It was one of the greatest doings of the kind that the mistress had in the whole course of the year, and the value of things intrusted to Jeanie's care was not to be told, at least so said Mrs. Girdwood herself.

Jeanie, and Marion Sapples, the washer-woman, with a pickle tea and sugar tied in the corners of a napkin, and two measured glasses of whisky in an old doctor's bottle, had been sent with the foul clothes the night before to the washing-house, and by break of day they were up and at their work; nothing particular, as Marion said, was observed about Jeanie till after they had taken their breakfast, when, in spreading out the clothes on the Green, some of the ne'er-do-weel young clerks of the town were seen gaffawing and haverelling[2] with Jeanie, the consequence of which was, that all the rest of the day she was light-headed; indeed, as Mrs. Girdwood told me herself, when Jeanie came in from the Green for Marion's dinner, she could na help remarking to her goodman, that there was something fey about the lassie, or, to use her own words, there was a storm in her tail, light where it might. But little did she think it was to bring the dule it did to her.

Jeanie having gotten the pig[3] with the wonted allowance of broth and beef in it for Marion, returned to the Green, and while Marion was eating the same, she disappeared. Once away, aye away; hilt or hair[4] of Jeanie was not seen that night. Honest Marion Sapples worked like a Trojan to the gloaming, but the light latheron[5] never came back; at last, seeing no other help for it, she got one of the other women at the washing-house to go to Mrs. Girdwood and to let her know what had happened, and how the best part of the washing would, unless help was sent, be obliged to lie out all night.

The deacon's wife well knew the great stake she had on that occasion in the boyne, and was for a season demented with the thought, but at last summoning her three daughters, and borrowing our lass, and Mr. Smeddum the tobacconist's niece, she went to the Green, and got every thing safely housed, yet still Jeanie Tirlet never made her appearance.

Mrs. Girdwood and her daughters having returned home, in a most uneasy state of mind on the lassie's account, the deacon himself came over to me, to consult what he ought to do as the head of a family. But I advised him to wait till Jeanie cast up, which was the next morning. Where she had been, and who she was with, could never be delved out of her, but the deacon brought her to the clerk's chamber, before Bailie Kittlewit, who was that day acting magistrate, and he sentenced her to be dismissed from her servitude with no more than the wage she had actually earned. The lassie was conscious of the ill turn she had played, and would have submitted in modesty; but one of the writers' clerks, an impudent whippersnapper, that had more to say with her than I need to say, bade her protest and appeal against the interlocutor, which the daring gipsey, so egged on, actually did, and the appeal next court day came before me. Whereupon, I knowing the outs and inns of the case, decerned that she should be fined five shillings to the poor of the parish, and ordained to go back to Mrs. Girdwood's, and there stay out the term of her servitude, or failing by refusal so to do, to be sent to prison, and put to hard labour for the remainder of the term.

Every body present, on hearing the circumstances, thought this a most judicious and lenient sentence, but so thought not the other servant lasses of the town; for in the evening, as I was going home, thinking no harm, on passing the Crosswell,[1] where a vast congregation of them were assembled with their stoups, discoursing the news of the day, they opened on me like a pack of hounds at a tod,[2] and I verily believed they would have mobbed me had I not made the best of my way home. My wife had been at the window when the hobbleshow began, and was just like to die of diversion at seeing me so set upon by the tinklers; and when I entered the dining-room she said, 'Really, Mr. Pawkie, ye're a gallant man, to be so weel in the good graces of the ladies.' But although I have often since had many a good laugh at the sport, I was not overly pleased with Mrs. Pawkie at the time— particularly as the matter between the deacon's wife and Jeanie did not end with my interlocutor. For the latheron's friend in the court having discovered that I had not decerned she was to do any work to Mrs. Girdwood, but only to stay out her term, advised her to do nothing when she went back, but go to her bed, which she was bardy[1] enough to do, until my poor friend, the deacon, in order to get a quiet riddance of her, was glad to pay her full fee, and board wages for the remainder of her time. This was the same Jeanie Tirlet that was transported for some misdemeanour, after making both Glasgow and Edinburgh owre het[2] to hold her.

CHAPTER XXXIX

THE NEWSPAPER

SHORTLY after the foregoing tribulation, of which I cannot take it upon me to say that I got so well rid, as of many other vexations of a more grievous nature, there arose a thing in the town, that caused to me much deep concern, and very serious reflection. I had been from the beginning, a true government man, as all loyal subjects ought in duty to be; for I never indeed could well understand how it would advantage, either the king or his ministers, to injure and do detriment to the lieges; on the contrary, I always saw and thought, that His Majesty, and those of his cabinet, had as great an interest in the prosperity and well-doing of the people, as it was possible for a landlord to have in the thriving of his tenantry. Accordingly, giving on all occasions, and at all times and seasons, even when the policy of the kingdom was overcast with a cloud, the King and Government, in church and state, credit for the best intentions, however humble their capacity in performance might seem in those straits and difficulties, which, from time to time, dumb-foundered the wisest in power and authority, I was exceedingly troubled to hear that a newspaper was to be set up in the borough, and that too by hands, not altogether clean of the coom[1] of jacobinical democracy.

The person that first brought me an account of this, and it was in a private confidential manner, was Mr. Scudmyloof, the grammar school-master, a man of method and lear,[2] to whom the fathers of the project had applied for an occasional cast of his skill, in the way of latin head-pieces, and essays of erudition concerning the free spirit among the ancient Greeks and Romans; but he, not liking the principle of the men concerned in the scheme, thought that it would be a public service to the community at large, if a stop could be put, by my help, to the opening of such an ettering[3] sore and king's evil as a newspaper, in our heretofore and hitherto truly royal and loyal borough; especially as it was given out that the calamity, for I can call it no less, was to be conducted on liberal principles, meaning, of course, in the most afflicting and vexatious manner towards His Majesty's ministers.

'What ye say,' said I to Mr. Scudmyloof when he told me the news, 'is very alarming, very much so indeed; but as there is no law yet actually and peremptorily prohibiting the sending forth of newspapers, I doubt it will not be in my power to interfere.'

He was of the same opinion; and we both agreed it was a rank exuberance of liberty, that the commonality should be exposed to the risk of being inoculated with anarchy and confusion, from what he, in his learned manner, judiciously called the predelictions of amateur pretension. The parties engaged in the project being Mr. Absolom the writer[4]—a man no overly reverential in his opinion of the law and Lords[5] when his clients lost their pleas, which, poor folk, was very often—and some three or four young and inexperienced lads, that were wont to read essays, and debate[1] the kittle points of divinity, and other hidden knowledge in the Cross Keys monthly, denying the existence of the soul of man, as Dr. Sinney told me, till they were deprived of all rationality by foreign or British spirits. In short, I was perplexed when I heard of the design, not knowing what to do, or what might be expected from me by government in a case of such emergency, as the setting up of a newspaper, so declaredly adverse to every species of vested trust and power; for it was easy to foresee, that those immediately on the scene, would be the first opposed to the onset and brunt of the battle. Never can any public man have a more delicate task imposed upon him, than to steer clear of offence in such a predicament. After a full consideration of the business, Mr. Scudmyloof declared that he would retire from the field, and stand aloof, and he rehearsed a fine passage in the Greek language on that head, pat to the occasion, but which I did not very thoroughly understand, being no deacon[2] in the dead languages, as I told him at the time.

But when the dominie had left me, I considered with myself, and having long before then observed, that our hopes, when realized, are always light in the grain, and our fears, when come to pass, less than they seemed as seen through the mists of time and distance, I resolved with myself to sit still with my eyes open, watching and saying nothing, and it was well that I deported myself so prudently; for when the first number of the paper made its appearance, it was as poor a job as ever was 'open to all parties, and influenced by none,' and it required but two eyes to discern, that there was no need of any strong power from the Lord Advocate to suppress or abolish the undertaking; for there was neither bir nor smeddum[3] enough in it, to molest the high, or to pleasure the low, so being left to itself, and not ennobled by any prosecution, as the schemers expected, it became as foisonless as the London Gazette on ordinary occasions. Those behind the curtain, who thought to bounce out with a grand stot[1] and strut before the world, finding that even I used it as a convenient vehicle to advertise my houses when need was, and which I did by the way of a canny seduction of policy, joking civilly with Mr. Absolom, anent his paper trumpet as I called it, they were utterly vanquished by seeing themselves of so little account in the world, and forsook the thing altogether; by which means it was gradually transformed into a very solid and decent supporter of the government—Mr. Absolom for his pains, being invited to all our public dinners, of which he gave full account, to the great satisfaction of all who were present; but more particularly to those who were not, especially the wives and ladies of the town, to whom it was a great pleasure to see the names of their kith and kin in print. And, indeed, to do Mr. Absolom justice, he was certainly at great pains to set off every thing to the best advantage, and usually put speeches to some of our names, which showed that, in the way of grammaticals, he was even able to have mended some of the parliamentary clish-maclavers, of which the Londoners, with all their skill in the craft, are so seldom able to lick into any shape of common sense.

Thus, by a judicious forbearance in the first instance, and a canny wising[2] towards the undertaking in the second, did I in the third, help to convert this dangerous political adversary, into a very respectable instrument of governmental influence and efficacy.

CHAPTER XL

THE SCHOOL-HOUSE SCHEME

THE spirit of opposition that kithed[3] towards me in the affair of Robin Boss, the drummer, was but an instance and symptom of the new nature then growing up in public matters. I was not long done with my second provostry, when I had occasion to congratulate myself on having passed twice through the dignity with so much respect. For, at the Michaelmas term, we had chosen Mr. Robert Plan into the vacancy caused by the death of that easy man, Mr. Weezle, which happened a short time before. I know not what came over me, that Mr. Plan was allowed to be chosen, for I never could abide him; being, as he was, a great stickler for small particularities, more zealous than discreet, and ever more intent to carry his own point, than to consider the good that might flow from a more urbane spirit. Not, that the man was devoid of ability; few, indeed, could set forth a more plausible tale; but he was continually meddling, keeking,[1] and poking, and always taking up a suspicious opinion of every body's intents and motives but his own. He was, besides, of a retired and sedentary habit of body; and the vapour of his stomach, as he was sitting by himself, often mounted into his upper story, and begat with his over zealous and meddling imagination, many unsound and fantastical notions. For all that, however, it must be acknowledged that Mr. Plan was a sincere honest man, only he sometimes lacked the discernment of the right from the wrong; and the consequence was, that, when in error, he was even more obstinate than when in the right; for his jealousy of human nature made him interpret falsely the heat with which his own headstrong zeal, when in error, was ever very properly resisted.

In nothing, however, did his molesting temper cause so much disturbance, as when in the year 1809, the bigging of the new school-house was under consideration. There was, about that time, a great sough throughout the country on the subject of education; and it was a fashion, to call schools academies; and out of a delusion rising from the use of that term, to think it necessary to decry the good plain old places,[2] wherein so many had learnt those things by which they helped to make the country and kingdom what it is, and to scheme for the ways and means to raise more edificial structures and receptacles. None was more infected with this distempretature than Mr. Plan; and, accordingly, when he came to the council-chamber, on the day that the matter of the new school-house was to be discussed, he brought with him a fine castle in the air, which he pressed hard upon us; representing, that if we laid out two or three thousand pounds more than we intended, and built a beautiful academy[1] and got a rector thereto, with a liberal salary and other suitable masters, opulent people at a distance, yea, gentlemen in the East and West Indies, would send their children to be educated among us; by which, great fame and profit would redound to the town.

Nothing could be more plausibly set forth; and, certainly, the project, as a notion, had many things to recommend it; but we had no funds adequate to undertake it, so, on the score of expence, knowing, as I did, the state of the public income, I thought it my duty to oppose it *in toto*; which fired Mr. Plan to such a degree, that he immediately insinuated, that I had some end of my own to serve in objecting to his scheme; and, because the wall that it was proposed to big[2] round the moderate building which we were contemplating, would inclose a portion of the backside of my new steading, at the Westergate,[3] he made no scruple of speaking, in a circumbendibus manner, as to the particular reasons that I might have for preferring it to his design, which he roused, in his way, as more worthy of the state of the arts and the taste of the age.

It was not easy to sit still under his imputations; especially, as I could plainly see, that some of the other members of the 'council leant towards his way of thinking. Nor will I deny, that in preferring the more moderate design, I had a contemplation of my own advantage in the matter of the dyke; for I do not think it any shame to a public man, to serve his own interests by those of the community, when he can righteously do so.

It was a thing never questionable, that the school-house required the inclosure of a wall, and the outside of that wall was of a natural necessity constrained to be a wing of inclosure to the ground beyond. Therefore, I see not how a corrupt motive ought to have been imputed to me, merely because I had a piece of ground that marched with the spot whereon it was intended to construct the new building; which spot, I should remark, belonged to the town before I bought mine. However, Mr. Plan so worked upon this material, that, what with one thing and what with another, he got the council persuaded to give up the moderate plan, and to consent to sell the ground where it had been proposed to build the new school, and to apply the proceeds towards the means of erecting a fine academy on the Green.

It was not easy to thole¹ to be so thwarted, especially for such an extravagant problem, by one so new to our councils and deliberations. I never was more fashed² in my life; for having hitherto, in all my plans for the improvement of the town, not only succeeded, but given satisfaction, I was vexed to see the council run away with such a speculative vagary. No doubt, the popular fantasy anent education and academies, had quite as muckle to do in the matter, as Mr. Plan's fozy³ rhetoric; but what availed that to me, at seeing a reasonable undertaking reviled and set aside, and grievous debts about to be laid on the community for a bubble as unsubstantial as that of the Ayr Bank.⁴ Besides, it was giving the upper hand in the council to Mr. Plan, to which, as a new man, he had no right. I said but little, for I saw it would be of no use; I, however, took a canny opportunity of remarking to old Mr. Dinledoup, the English teacher,⁵ that this castle-building scheme of an academy would cause great changes probably in the masters; and as, no doubt, it would oblige us to adopt the new methods of teaching, I would like to have a private inkling of what salary he would expect on being superannuated.

The worthy man was hale and hearty, not exceeding three

score and seven,[1] and had never dreamt of being superannuated. He was, besides, a prideful bodie, and, like all of
his calling, thought not a little of himself. The surprise,
therefore, with which he heard me was just wonderful. For a
space of time, he stood still and uttered nothing; then he took
his snuff-box out of the flap pocket of his waistcoat, where he
usually carried it, and giving three distinct and very comical
raps, drew his mouth into a purse. 'Mr. Pawkie,' at last he
said; 'Mr. Pawkie, there will be news in the world before I
consent to be superannuated.'

This was what I expected, and I replied, 'Then, why do
not you and Mr. Scudmyloof, of the grammar school,
represent to the magistrates, that the present school-house
may, with a small repair, serve for many years.' And, so I
sowed an effectual seed of opposition to Mr. Plan, in a quarter
he never dreamt of. For the two dominees, in the dread of
undergoing some transmogrification, laid their heads together,
and went round among the parents of the children, and
decryed the academy project, and the cess that the cost of it
would bring upon the town; by which a public opinion was
begotten and brought to a bearing, that the magistrates could
not resist; so the old school-house was repaired, and Mr.
Plan's scheme, as well as the other, given up. In this, it is true,
if I had not the satisfaction to get a dyke to the backside of
my property, I had the pleasure to know, that my interloping
adversary was disappointed; the which was a sort of com-
pensation.

CHAPTER XLI

BENEFITS OF NEUTRALITY

THE general election in 1812 was a source of trouble and
uneasiness to me; both because our district of boroughs was
to be contested, and because the contest was not between men

of opposite principles, but of the same side. To neither of
them had I any particular leaning; on the contrary, I would
have preferred the old member, whom I had, on different
occasions, found an accessible and tractable instrument, in
the way of getting small favours with the government and
India company, for friends that never failed to consider them
as such things should be. But what could I do? Providence
had placed me in the van of the battle, and I needs must
fight; so thought every body, and so for a time I thought
myself. Weighing, however, the matter one night soberly in
my mind, and seeing that whichever of the two candidates
was chosen, I, by my adherent loyalty to the cause for which
they were both declared, the contest between them being a
rivalry of purse and personality, would have as much to say
with the one as with the other, came to the conclusion that it
was my prudentest course, not to intermeddle at all in the
election. Accordingly, as soon as it was proper to make a
declaration of my sentiments, I made this known, and it
caused a great wonderment in the town; nobody could
imagine it possible that I was sincere, many thinking there
was something aneath it, which would kithe in time to the
surprise of the public. However, the peutering[1] went on, and
I took no part. The two candidates were as civil and as
liberal, the one after the other, to Mrs. Pawkie and my
daughters, as any gentlemen of a parliamentary understanding could be. Indeed, I verily believe, that although I had
been really chosen delegate,[2] as it was at one time intended
I should be, I could not have hoped for half the profit that
came in from the dubiety which my declaration of neutrality
caused; for as often as I assured the one candidate, that I did
not intend even to be present at the choosing of the delegate,
some rich present was sure to be sent to my wife, of which the
other no sooner heard than he was upsides with him. It was
just a sport to think of me protesting my neutrality, and to see
how little I was believed. For still the friends of the two
candidates, like the figures of the four quarters of the world

round Britannia in a picture,[1] came about my wife, and poured into her lap a most extraordinary paraphanalia from the horn of their abundance.

The common talk of the town was, that surely I was bereft of my wonted discretion, to traffic so openly with corruption; and that it could not be doubted I would have to face the House of Commons, and suffer the worst pains and penalties of bribery. But what did all this signify to me, who was conscious of the truth and integrity of my motives and intents? 'They say—what say they?—let them say'—was what I said, as often as any of my canny friends came to me; saying, 'for God's sake, Mr. Pawkie, tak' tent.'[2] 'I hope, Mr. Pawkie, ye ken the ground ye stand on;' or, 'I wish that some folks were aware of what's said about them.' In short, I was both angered and diverted by their clishmaclavers, and having some need to go into Glasgow, just on the eve of the election, I thought I would, for diversion, give them something in truth to play with; so saying nothing to my shop lad the night before, nor even to Mrs. Pawkie, (for the best of women are given to tattling,) till we were in our beds, I went off early on the morning of the day appointed for choosing the delegate.

The consternation in the town at my evasion was wonderful. Nobody could fathom it, and the friends and supporters of the rival candidates looked, as I was told, at one another, in a state of suspicion that was just a curiosity to witness. Even when the delegate was chosen, every body thought that something would be found wanting, merely because I was not present. The new member himself, when his election was declared, did not feel quite easy; and, more than once, when I saw him after my return from Glasgow, he said to me, in a particular manner: 'but tell me now, Bailie, what was the true reason of your visit to Glasgow?' And, in like manner, his opponent also hinted, that he would petition against the return; but there were some facts which he could not well get at without my assistance; insinuating, that I might find my account in helping him.

At last, the true policy of the part I had played began to be understood, and I got far more credit for the way in which I had turned both parties, so well to my own advantage, than if I had been the means of deciding the election by my single vote.

CHAPTER XLII

THE NEW MEMBER

BUT the new member was, in some points, not of so tractable a nature as many of his predecessors had been; and notwithstanding all the couthy jocosity and curry-favouring of his demeanour towards us before the election, he was no sooner returned, than he began, as it were, to snap his fingers in the very faces of those of the council to whom he was most indebted, which was a thing not of very easy endurance, considering how they had taxed their consciences in his behalf; and this treatment was the more bitterly felt, as the old member had been, during the whole of his time, as considerate and obliging as could reasonably be expected; doing any little job that needed his helping hand when it was in his power; and when it was not, replying to our letters in a most discreet and civil manner. To be sure, poor man, he had but little to say in the way of granting favours, for being latterly inclined to a whiggish principle, he was, in consequence, debarred from all manner of government patronage, and had little in his gift but soft words and fair promises. Indeed, I have often remarked, in the course of my time, that there is a surprising difference, in regard to the urbanities in use among those who have not yet come to authority, or who have been cast down from it, and those who are in the full possession of the rule and domination of office; but never was the thing plainer, than in the conduct of the new member.

He was by nature and inclination one of the upsetting[1]

sort; a kind of man, who in all manner of business, have a leaven of contrariness, that makes them very hard to deal with; and he, being conjunct with His Majesty's ministers at London, had imbibed and partook of that domineering spirit, to which all men are ordained, to be given over whenever they are clothed in the garments of power. Many among us thought, by his colleaguing with the government, that we had got a great catch, and they were both blithe and vogie[1] when he was chosen; none doubting but he would do much good servitude to the corporation, and the interests of the borough. However he soon gave a rebuff, that laid us all on our backs in a state of the greatest mortification. But although it behoved me to sink down with the rest, I was but little hurt; on the contrary, I had a good laugh in my sleeve at the time; and afterwards, many a merry tumbler of toddy with my brethren, when they had recovered from their discomfiture. The story was this:—

About a fortnight after the election, Mr. Scudmyloof, the school-master, called one day on me, in my shop, and said, 'That being of a nervous turn, the din of the school did not agree with him; and that he would, therefore, be greatly obligated to me, if I would get him made a gauger.'[2] There had been something in the carriage of our new member before he left the town, that was not satisfactory to me; forbye,[3] my part at the election, the which made me loth to be the first to ask for any grace, though the master was a most respectable and decent man; so I advised Mr. Scudmyloof to apply to Provost Pickandab, who had been the delegate, as the person to whose instrumentality the member was most obliged; and to whose application, he, of course, would pay the greatest attention.

Whether Provost Pickandab had made any observe similar to mine, I never could rightly understand, though I had a notion to that effect; he, however, instead of writing himself, made the application for Mr. Scudmyloof an affair of the council; recommending him as a worthy modest man, which he really was, and well qualified for the post. Off went this notable letter, and by return of post from London, we got our answer as we were all sitting in council, deliberating anent the rebuilding of the Cross-well,[1] which had been for some time in a sore state of dilapidation; and, surely, never was any letter more to the point and less to the purpose of an applicant. It was very short and pithy, just acknowledging receipt of ours; and adding thereto, 'circumstances do not allow me to pay any attention to such applications.' We all, with one accord, in sympathy and instinct, threw ourselves back in our chairs at the words, looking at Provost Pickandab, with the pragmatical epistle in his hand, sitting in his place at the head of the table, with the countenance of consternation.

When I came to myself, I began to consider, that there must have been something no right in the Provost's own letter on the subject, to cause such an uncourteous rebuff; so after condemning, in very strong terms, the member's most ungenteel style, in order to procure for myself a patient hearing, I warily proposed, that the Provost's application should be read, a copy thereof being kept, and I had soon a positive confirmation of my suspicion. For the Provost, being fresh in the dignity of his office, and naturally of a prideful turn, had addressed the parliament man as if he was under an obligation to him; and as if the council had a right to command him to get the gauger's post, or, indeed, any other for whomsoever they might apply. So, seeing whence the original sin of the affair had sprung, I said nothing; but the same night I wrote a humiliated letter from myself to the member, telling him how sorry we all were for the indiscretion that had been used towards him, and how much it would pleasure me, to heal the breach that had happened between him and the borough, with other words of an oily and conciliating policy.

The indignant member, by the time my letter reached hand, had cooled in his passion, and, I fancy, was glad of an occasion to do away the consequence of the rupture; for with a most extraordinary alacrity he procured Mr. Scudmyloof the post, writing me, when he had done so, in the civilest manner, and saying many condescending things concerning his regard for me; all which ministered to maintain and uphold my repute and consideration in the town, as superior to that of the provost.

CHAPTER XLIII

MY THIRD PROVOSTRY

IT was at the Michaelmas 1813 that I was chosen Provost for the third time, and at the special request of My Lord the Earl, who, being in ill health, had been advised by the faculty of doctors in London to try the medicinal virtues of the air and climate of Sicily, in the Mediterranean Sea; and there was an understanding on the occasion, that I should hold the post of honour for two years, chiefly in order to bring to a conclusion different works that the town had then in hand.

At the two former times, when I was raised to the dignity, and, indeed, at all times, when I received any advancement, I had enjoyed an elation of heart, and was, as I may say, crouse and vogie;[1] but experience had worked a change upon my nature, and when I was saluted on my election with the customary greetings and gratulations of those present, I felt a solemnity enter into the frame of my thoughts, and I became as it were a new man on the spot. When I returned home to my own house, I retired into my private chamber for a time, to consult with myself in what manner my deportment should be regulated; for I was conscious that heretofore I had been overly governed with a disposition to do things my own way, and although not in an avaricious temper, yet something, I must confess, with a sort of sinister respect for my own interests. It may be, that standing now clear and free of the world, I had less incitement to be so grippy,[2] and so was thought of me, I very well know; but in sobriety and truth I conscientiously affirm, and herein record, that I had lived to partake of the purer spirit which the great mutations of the age had conjured into public affairs, and I saw that there was a necessity to carry into all dealings with the concerns of the community, the same probity which helps a man to prosperity, in the sequestered traffic of private life.

This serious and religious communing wrought within me to a benign and pleasant issue, and when I went back in the afternoon to dine with the corporation in the council room, and looked around me on the bailies, the counsellors and the deacons, I felt as if I was indeed elevated above them all, and that I had a task to perform, in which I could hope for but little sympathy from many; and the first thing I did was to measure, with a discreet hand, the festivity of the occasion.

At all former and precedent banquets, it had been the custom to give vent to meickle wanton and luxurious indulgence, and to galravitch both at hack and manger,[1] in a very expensive manner to the funds of the town. I, therefore, resolved to set my face against this for the future; and accordingly, when we had enjoyed a jocose temperance of loyalty and hilarity, with a decent measure of wine, I filled a glass, and requesting all present to do the same, without any preliminary reflections on the gavaulling[2] of past times, I drank good afternoon to each severally, and then rose from the table, in a way that put an end to all the expectations of more drink.

But this conduct did not give satisfaction to some of the old hands, who had been for years in the habit and practice of looking forward to the provost's dinner, as to a feast of fat things. Mr. Peevie, one of the very sickerest of all the former sederunts,[3] came to me next morning, in a remonstrating disposition, to enquire what had come over me, and to tell me that every body was much surprised, and many thought it not right of me to break in upon ancient and wonted customs in such a sudden and unconcerted manner.

This Mr. Peevie was, in his person, a stumpy man, well advanced in years. He had been, in his origin, a bonnet-maker, but falling heir to a friend[1] that left him a property, he retired from business about the fiftieth year of his age, doing nothing, but walking about with an ivory headed staff, in a suit of dark blue cloth, with yellow buttons, wearing a large cocked hat, and a white three-tiered wig, which was well powdered every morning by Duncan Curl, the barber. The method of his discourse and conversation was very precise, and his words were all set forth in a style of consequence, that took with many for a season, as the pith and marrow of solidity and sense. The bodie, however, was but a pompous trifle, and I had for many a day held his observes and admonishments in no very reverential estimation. So that when I heard him address me, in such a memorializing manner, I was inclined and tempted to set him off with a flea in his lug. However, I was enabled to bridle and rein in this prejudicial humour, and answer him in his own way.

'Mr. Peevie,' quo' I, 'you know that few in the town hae the repute that ye hae for a gift of sagacity by common,[2] and, therefore, I'll open my mind to you in this matter, with a frankness that would not be a judicious polity with folk of a lighter understanding.'

This was before the counter in my shop. I then walked in behind it, and drew the chair, that stands in the corner nearer to the fire, for Mr. Peevie. When he was seated thereon, and, as was his wont in conversation, had placed both his hands on the top of his staff, and leant his chin on the same, I subjoined,

'Mr. Peevie, I need not tell to a man of your experience, that folk in public stations cannot always venture to lay before the world the reasons of their conduct on particular occasions, and, therefore, when men who have been long in the station that I have filled in this town, are seen to step aside from what has been in time past, it is to be hoped that grave and sensible persons like you, Mr. Peevie, will no rashly condemn them unheard; nevertheless, my good friend, I am very happy that ye have spoken to me anent the stinted allowance of wine and punch at the dinner, because the like thing from any other would have made me jealouse[1] that the complaint was altogether owing to a disappointed appetite, which is a corrupt thing, that I am sure would never affect a man of such a public spirit as you are well known to be.'

Mr. Peevie, at this, lifted his chin from off his hands, and dropping his arms down upon his knees, held his staff by the middle, as he replied looking upward to me.

'What ye say, Provost Pawkie, has in it a solid commodity of judgment and sensibility; and ye may be sure, that I was not without a cogitation of reflection, that there had been a discreet argument of economy at the bottom of the revolution, which was brought to a criticism yesterday's afternoon. Weel aware am I, that men in authority cannot appease and quell the inordinate concupiscence of the multitude, and that in a' stations of life there are persons, who would mumpileese[2] the retinue of the King and Government for their own behoof and eeteration, without any regard to the cause or effect of such manifest predelictions. But ye do me no more than a judicature, in supposing that, in this matter, I am habituated wi' the best intentions. For I can assure you, Mr. Pawkie, that no man in this community has a more literal respect for your character than I have, or is more disposed for a judicious example of continence in the way of public enterteenment than I have ever been; for, as you know, I am of a constipent principle towards every extravagant and costive outlay. Therefore, on my own account, I had a satisfaction at seeing the abridgement which you made of our former inebrieties; but there are other persons of a conjugal nature, who look upon such castrations as a deficiency of their rights, and the like of them will find fault with the best procedures.'

'Very true, Mr. Peevie,' said I, 'that's very true; but if His Majesty's government, in this war for all that is dear to us as men and Britons, wish us, who are in authority under them, to pare and save, in order that the means of bringing the war to a happy end may not be wasted, an example must be set, and that example, as a loyal subject and a magistrate, it's my intent so to give, in the hope and confidence of being backed by every person of a right way of thinking.'

'It's no to be deputed, Provost Pawkie,' replied my friend, somewhat puzzled by what I had said; 'it's no to be deputed, that we live in a gigantic vortex, and that every man is bound to make an energetic dispensation for the good of his country; but I could not have thought that our means had come to sic an alteration and extremity, as that the reverent homage of the Michaelmas dinners could have been enacted, and declared absolute and abolished, by any interpolation less than the omnipotence of parliament.'

'Not abolished, Mr. Peevie,' cried I, interrupting him; 'that would indeed be a stretch of power. No, no; I hope we're both ordained to partake of many a Michaelmas dinner thegether yet; but with a meted measure of sobriety. For we neither live in the auld time nor the golden age, and it would not do now for the like of you and me, Mr. Peevie, to be seen in the dusk of the evening, toddling home from the town-hall wi' gogling een and havering tongues, and one of the town-officers following at a distance in case of accidents; sic things, ye ken, hae been, but no body would plead for their continuance.'

Mr. Peevie did not relish this, for in truth it came near his own doors, it having been his annual practice for some years at the Michaelmas dinner to give a sixpence to James Hound, the officer, to see him safe home, and the very time before he had sat so long, that honest James was obligated to cleek and oxter him[1] the whole way; and in the way home, the old man, cagie[2] with what he had gotten, stood in the causey opposite to Mr. M'Vest's door, then deacon of the taylors, and trying to snap his fingers, sang like a daft-man,

> The sheets they were thin and the blankets were sma',
> And the taylor fell through the bed, thimble and a'.

So that he was disconcerted by my inuendo, and shortly after

left the shop, I trow, with small inclination to propagate any
sedition against me, for the abbreviation I had made of the
Michaelmas galravitching.[1]

CHAPTER XLIV

THE CHURCH VACANT

I HAD long been sensible that in getting Mr. Pittle the Kirk,
I had acted with the levity and indiscretion of a young man.
But at that time, I understood not the nature of public trust,
nor indeed did the community at large. Men in power then
ruled more for their own ends, than in these latter times, and
use and wont sanctioned and sanctified many doings, from
the days of our ancestors, that but to imagine will astonish and
startle posterity. Accordingly, when Mr. Pittle, after a linger-
ing illness, was removed from us, which happened in the first
year of my third provostry, I bethought me of the consequences which had ensued from his presentation, and resolved
within myself to act a very different part in the filling up of the
vacancy. With this intent, as soon as the breath was out of his
body, I sent round for some of the most weighty and best
considered of the counsellors and elders, and told them that a
great trust was, by the death of the minister, placed in our
hands, and that, in these times, we ought to do what in us lay
to get a shepherd, that would gather back to the establishment
the flock which had been scattered among the seceders, by the
feckless crook, and ill-guiding of their former pastor.

They all agreed with me in this, and named one eminent
divine after another; but the majority of voices were in favour
of Dr. Whackdeil, of Kirkbogle, a man of weight and example,
both in and out the pulpit, so that it was resolved to give the
call to him, which was done accordingly.

It however came out that the Kirkbogle stipend was better

than ours, and the consequence was, that having given the call, it became necessary to make up the deficiency, for it was not reasonable to expect that the Reverend Doctor, with his small family of nine children, would remove to us at a loss. How to accomplish this was a work of some difficulty, for the town revenues were all eaten up with one thing and another; but upon an examination of the income, arising from what had been levied on the seats for the repair of the church, it was discovered that, by doing away a sinking fund, which had been set apart to redeem the debt incurred for the same, and by the town taking the debt on itself, we could make up a sufficiency to bring the Doctor among us. And in so far as having an orthodox preacher, and a very excellent man for our minister, there was great cause to be satisfied with that arrangement.

But the payment of the interest on the public debt, with which the town was burdened, began soon after to press heavily on us, and we were obligated to take on more borrowed money, in order to keep our credit, and likewise to devise ways and means, in the shape of public improvements, to raise an income to make up what was required. This led me to suggest the building of the new bridge, the cost of which, by contract, there was no reason to complain of, and the toll thereon,[1] while the war lasted, not only paid the interest of the borrowed money, by which it was built, but left a good penny in the nook of the Treasurer's box for other purposes.

Had the war continued, and the nation to prosper thereby as it did, nobody can doubt, that a great source of wealth and income was opened to the town; but when peace came round, and our prosperity began to fall off,[2] the traffic on the bridge grew less and less, insomuch that the toll, as I now understand, (for since my resignation, I meddle not with public concerns,) does not yield enough to pay the five per cent. on the prime cost of the bridge, by which my successors suffer much molestation in raising the needful money to do the same. However, every body continues well satisfied with Doctor Whackdeil, who was the original cause of this perplexity, and it is to be hoped that, in time, things will grow better, and the revenues come round again to indemnify the town for its present tribulation.

CHAPTER XLV

THE STRAMASH[1] IN THE COUNCIL

As I have said, my third provostry was undertaken in a spirit of sincerity, different, in some degree, from that of the two former; but strange and singular as it may seem, I really think I got less credit for the purity of my intents, than I did even in the first. During the whole term from the election in the year 1813 to the Michaelmas following, I verily believe that no one proposal which I made to the council was construed in a right sense; this was partly owing to the repute I had acquired for canny management, but chiefly to the perverse views and misconceptions of that Yanky thorn-in-the-side, Mr. Hickery, who never desisted from setting himself against every thing that sprang from me, and as often found some show of plausibility to maintain his argumentations. And yet, for all that, he was a man held in no esteem or respect in the town, for he had wearied every body out by his everlasting contradictions. Mr. Plan was likewise a source of great tribulation to me, for he was ever and anon coming forward with some new device, either for ornament or profit, as he said, to the borough; and no small portion of my time, that might have been more advantageously employed, was wasted in the thriftless consideration of his schemes: all which, with my advanced years, begat in me a sort of distate to the bickerings of the council chamber; so I conferred and communed with myself, anent the possibility of ruling the town without having recourse to so unwieldy a vehicle as the wheels within wheels of the factions which the Yanky reformator, and that projectile, Mr. Plan, as he was called by Mr. Peevie, had inserted among us.

I will no equivocate that there was, in this notion an appearance of taking more on me than the laws allowed, but then my motives were so clean to my conscience, and I was so sure of satisfying the people by the methods I intended to pursue, that there could be no moral fault in the trifle of illegality, which, may be, I might have been led on to commit. —However, I was fortunately spared from the experiment, by a sudden change in the council.—One day Mr. Hickery, and Mr. Plan, who had been for years colleaguing together for their own ends, happened to differ in opinion, and the one suspecting that this difference was the fruit of some secret corruption, they taunted each other, and came to high words, and finally to an open quarrel, actually shaking their neeves[1] across the table, and, I'll no venture to deny, may be exchanging blows.

Such a convulsion in the sober councils of a borough town was never heard of. It was a thing not to be endured, and so I saw at the time, and was resolved to turn it to the public advantage. Accordingly, when the two angry men had sat back in their seats, bleached in the face with passion, and panting and out of breath, I rose up in my chair at the head of the table, and with a judicial solemnity addressed the council, saying, that what we had witnessed, was a disgrace not to be tolerated in a Christian land; that unless we obtained indemnity for the past, and security for the future, I would resign, but in doing so I would bring the cause thereof before the Fifteen at Edinburgh,[2] yea, even to the House of Lords at London; so I gave the offending parties notice, as well as those who, from motives of personal friendship, might be disposed to overlook the insult that had been given to the constituted authority of the King, so imperfectly represented in my person, as it would seem, by the audacious conflict and misdemeanour which had just taken place.

This was striking while the iron was hot: every one looked at my sternness with surprise, and some begged me to be seated, and to consider the matter calmly.—'Gentlemen,' quo' I, 'dinna mistake me. I never was in more composure all my life.—It's indeed no on my own account that I feel on this occasion. The gross violation of all the decent decorum of magisterial authority is not a thing that affects me in my own person; it's an outrage against the state; the prerogatives of the king's crown are endamaged; atonement must be made, or punishment must ensue. It's a thing that by no possibility can be overlooked: it's an offence committed in open court, and we cannot but take cognizance thereof.'

I saw that what I said was operating to an effect, and that the two troublesome members were confounded. Mr. Hickery rose to offer some apology; but, perceiving I had now got him in a girn,[1] I interposed my authority, and would not permit him to proceed.

'Mr. Hickery,' said I, 'it's of no use to address yourself to me. I am very sensible that ye are sorry for your fault, but that will not do; the law knows no such thing as repentance, and it is the law, not me, nor our worthy friends here, that ye have offended. In short, Mr. Hickery, the matter is such, that, in one word either you and Mr. Plan must quit your seats at this table of your own free-will, or I must quit mine, and mine I will not give up without letting the public know the shame on your part that has compelled me.'

He sat down and I sat down, and for some time the other counsellors looked at one another in silence and wonder. Seeing, however, that my gentle hint was not likely to be taken, I said to the town-clerk who was sitting at the bottom of the table,

'Sir, it's your duty to make a minute of every thing that is done and said at the sederunts of the council; and, as provost, I hereby require of you to record the particularities of this melancholy crisis.'

Mr. Keelevine made an endeavour to dissuade me, but I set him down with a stern voice, striking the table at the same time with all my bir,[2] as I said, 'Sir, you have no voice here.— Do you refuse to perform what I order? At your peril I command the thing to be done.'

Never had such austerity been seen in my conduct before. The whole council sat in astonishment, and Mr. Keelevine prepared his pen, and took a sheet of paper to draw out a notation of the minute; when Mr. Peevie rose, and after coughing three times, and looking first at me, and syne at the two delinquents, said,—

'My Lord Provost, I was surprised and beginning to be confounded at the explosion which the two gentlemen have committed.—No man can designate the extent of such an official malversation, demonstrated as it has been here in the presence of us all, who are the lawful custodiers of the kingly dignity in this His Majesty's royal borough. I will, therefore, not take it upon me either to apologise or to obliviate their offence; for, indeed, it is an offence that merits the most condign animadversion, and the consequences might be legible for ever, were a gentleman, so conspicable in the town as you are, to evacuate the magistracy on account of it. But it is my balsamic advice, that rather than promulge this matter, the two malcontents should abdicate, and that a precept should be placarded at this sederunt as if they were not here, but had resigned and evaded their places, precursive to the meeting.'

To this I answered, that no one could suspect me of wishing to push the matter further, provided the thing could be otherwise settled; and, therefore, if Mr. Plan and Mr. Hickery would shake hands and agree never to notice what had passed to each other, and the other members and magistrates would consent likewise to bury the business in oblivion, I would agree to the balsamic advice of Mr. Peevie, and even waive my obligation to bind over the hostile parties to keep the king's peace, so that the whole affair might neither be known, nor placed upon record.

Mr. Hickery, I could discern, was rather surprised; but I found that I had thus got the thief in the wuddy,[1] and he had no choice, so both he and Mr. Plan rose from their seats in a very sheepish manner, and looking at us as if they had unpleasant ideas in their minds, they departed forth the council chamber, and a minute was made by the town-clerk, that they, having resigned their trust as counsellors, two other gentlemen at the next meeting should be chosen into their stead.

Thus did I, in a manner most unexpected, get myself rid and clear of the two most obdurate oppositionists, and by taking care to choose discreet persons for their successors, I was enabled to wind the council round my finger, which was a far more expedient method of governing the community than what I had at one time meditated, even if I could have brought it to a bearing. But, in order to understand the full weight and importance of this, I must describe how the choice and election was made, because, in order to make my own power and influence the more sicker, it was necessary that I should not be seen in the business.

CHAPTER XLVI

THE NEW COUNSELLORS

MR. PEEVIE was not a little proud of the part he had played in the storm of the council, and his words grew, if possible, longer-nebbit and more kittle[1] than before; in so much, that the same evening when I called on him after dusk, by way of a device to get him to help the implementing of my intents with regard to the choice of two gentlemen to succeed those whom he called 'the expurgated dislocators,' it was with a great difficulty that I could expiscate his meaning. 'Mr. Peevie,' said I, when we were cosily seated by ourselves in his little back parlour, the mistress having set out the gardevin and tumblers, and the lass brought in the hot water—'I do not think, Mr. Peevie, that in all my experience, and I am now both an old man and an old magistrate, that I ever saw any thing better managed than the manner in which ye quelled the hobbleshow this morning, and therefore we maun hae a

little more of your balsamic advice, to make a' heal among us
again—and now that I think o't, how has it happent that ye
hae never been a Bailie. I'm sure its due both to your character
and circumstance that ye should take upon you a portion of the
burden of the town honours. Therefore, Mr. Peevie, would it
no be a very proper thing, in the choice of the new counsellors,
to take men of a friendly mind towards you, and of an easy
and manageable habit of will.'

The old man was mightily taken with this insinuation, and
acknowledged that it would give him pleasure to be a Bailie
next year. We then cannily proceeded, just as if one thing
begat another, to discourse anent the different men that were
likely to do as counsellors, and fixed at last on Alexander
Hodden, the blanket merchant, and Patrick Fegs, the grocer,
both excellent characters of their kind. There was not, indeed,
in the whole borough at the time, a person of such a flexible
easy nature as Mr. Hodden; and his neighbour, Mr. Fegs,
was even better, for he was so good-tempered, and kindly,
and complying, that the very callants[1] at the grammar-school
had nicknamed him Barley-sugar Pate.

'No better than them can be,' said I to Mr. Peevie; 'they
are likewise both well to do in the world, and should be
brought into consequence; and the way o't canna be in better
hands than your own. I would therefore recommend it to you
to see them on the subject, and if ye find them willing, lay your
hairs in the water[2] to bring the business to a bearing.'

Accordingly we settled to speak of it as a matter in part
decided, that Mr. Hodden and Mr. Fegs were to be the two
new counsellors; and to make the thing sure, as soon as I
went home, I told it to Mrs. Pawkie, as a state secret, and laid
my injunctions on her not to say a word about it, either to
Mrs. Hodden or to Mrs. Fegs, the wives of our two elect; for I
knew her disposition, and that although, to a certainty, not a
word of the fact would escape from her, yet she would be
utterly unable to rest until she had made the substance of it
known, in some way or another; and as I expected, so it came

to pass. She went that very night to Mrs. Rickerton, the mother of Mr. Fegs's wife, and, as I afterwards picked out of her, told the old lady, that may be, ere long, she would hear of some great honour that would come to her family, with other mystical intimations, that pointed plainly to the dignities of the magistracy; the which, when she had returned home, so worked upon the imagination of Mrs. Rickerton, that, before going to bed, she felt herself obliged to send for her daughter, to the end that she might be delivered and eased of what she had heard. In this way Mr. Fegs got a foretaste of what had been concerted for his advantage, and Mr. Peevie, in the mean time, through his helpmate had, in like manner, not been idle; the effect of all which was, that next day, every where in the town, people spoke of Mr. Hodden and Mr. Fegs as being ordained to be the new counsellors, in the stead of the two who had, as it was said, resigned in so unaccountable a manner. So that no candidates offered, and the election was concluded in the most candid and agreeable spirit possible;—after which I had neither trouble nor adversary, but went on, in my own prudent way, with the works in hand, the completion of the new bridge, the reparation of the tolbooth steeple, and the bigging of the new schools on the piece of ground adjoining to my own at the westergate; and in the doing of the latter job, I had an opportunity of manifesting my public spirit; for when the scheme, as I have related, was some years before given up, on account of Mr. Plan's castles in the air for educating tawney children from the East and West Indies, I inclosed my own ground, and built the house thereon, now occupied by Collector Gather's widow, and the town, per consequence, was not called on for one penny of the cost, but saved so much of a wall as the length of mine extended, a part not less than a full third part of the whole. No doubt, all these great and useful public works were not done without money, but the town was then in great credit, and many persons were willing and ready to lend, for every thing was in a prosperous order, and we had a prospect of a vast increase of income, not only from the toll on the new bridge, but likewise from three very excellent shops which we repaired on the ground floor of the tolbooth. We had likewise feued[1] out to advantage, a considerable portion of the town moor, so that had things gone on in the way they were in my time, there can be no doubt that the borough would have been in very flourishing circumstances; and, instead of being drowned, as it now is, in debt, it might have been in the most topping way; and if the project that I had formed for bringing in a supply of water by pipes,[2] had been carried into effect, it would have been a most advantageous undertaking for the community at large.

But my task is now drawing to an end, and I have only to relate what happened at the conclusion of the last act of my very serviceable and eventful life, the which I will proceed to do with as much brevity as is consistent with the nature of that free and faithful spirit in which the whole of their[3] notandums have been indited.

CHAPTER XLVII

THE RESIGNATION

SHORTLY after the battle of Waterloo, I began to see that a change was coming in among us. There was less work for the people to do, no outgate[4] in the army for roving and idle spirits, and those who had tacks of the town lands complained of slack markets; indeed, in my own double vocation of the cloth shop and wine cellar,[5] I had a taste and experience of the general declension that would of a necessity ensue, when the great outlay of government and the discharge from public employ drew more and more to an issue. So I bethought me, that being now well stricken in years, and, though I say it that should not, likewise a man in good respect and circumstances, it would be a prudent thing to retire and secede entirely from all farther intromissions with public affairs.

Accordingly, towards the midsummer of the year 1816, I commenced in a far off way to give notice, that at Michaelmas I intended to abdicate my authority and power, to which intimations little heed was at first given; but gradually the seed took with the soil, and began to swell and shoot up, in so much, that, by the middle of August, it was an understood thing that I was to retire from the council, and refrain entirely from the part I had so long played with credit in the borough.

When people first began to believe that I was in earnest, I cannot but acknowledge I was remonstrated with by many, and that not a few were pleased to say my resignation would be a public loss; but these expressions, and the disposition of them, wore away before Michaelmas came; and I had some sense of the feeling which the fluctuating gratitude of the multitude often causes to rise in the breasts of those who have ettled[1] their best to serve the ungrateful populace. However, I considered with myself that it would not do for me, after what I had done for the town and commonality to go out of office like a knotless thread, and that as a something was of right due to me, I would be committing an act of injustice to my family if I neglected the means of realizing the same. But it was a task of delicacy, and who could I prompt to tell the town council to do what they ought to do? I could not myself speak of my own services—I could ask nothing. Truly it was a subject that cost me no small cogitation, for I could not confide it even to the wife of my bosom. However, I gained my end, and the means and method thereof may advantage other public characters, in a similar strait, to know and understand.

Seeing that nothing was moving onward in men's minds to do the act of courtesy to me, so justly my due, on the Saturday before Michaelmas I invited Mr. Mucklewheel, the hosier, (who had the year before been chosen into the council, in the place of old Mr. Peevie, who had a paralytic, and never in consequence was made a bailie), to take a glass of toddy with me, a way and method of peutering[2] with the counsellors, one by one, that I often found of a great efficacy in bringing their understandings into a docile state, and when we had discussed one cheerer with the usual clishmaclaver of the times, I began, as we were both birzing[1] the sugar for the second, to speak with a circumbendibus about my resignation of the trusts I had so long held with profit to the community.

'Mr. Mucklewheel,' quo' I, 'ye're but a young man, and no versed yet, as ye will be, in the policy and diplomatics that are requisite in the management of the town, and therefore I need not say any thing to you about what I have got an inkling of, as to the intents of the new magistrates and council towards me. Its very true that I have been long a faithful servant to the public, but he's a weak man who looks to any reward from the people; and after the experience I have had, I would certainly prove myself to be one of the very weakest, if I thought it was likely, that either anent the piece of plate and the vote of thanks, any body would take a speciality of trouble.'

To this Mr. Mucklewheel answered, that he was glad to hear such a compliment was intended; 'No man,' said he, 'more richly deserves a handsome token of public respect, and I will surely give the proposal all the countenance and support in my power possible to do.'

'As to that,' I replied, pouring in the rum and helping myself to the warm water, 'I entertain no doubt, and I have every confidence that the proposal, when it is made, will be in a manner unanimously approved. But, Mr. Mucklewheel, what's every body's business, is nobody's. I have heard of no one that's to bring the matter forward; its all fair and smooth to speak of such things in holes and corners, but to face the public with them is another sort of thing. For few men can abide to see honours conferred on their neighbours, though, between ourselves, Mr. Mucklewheel, every man in a public trust should, for his own sake, further and promote the bestowing of public rewards on his predecessors; because looking forward to the time when he must himself become a predecessor, he should think how he would feel were he, like me, after a magistracy of near to fifty years, to sink into the humility of a private station, as if he had never been any thing in the world. In sooth, Mr. Mucklewheel, I'll no deny that it's a satisfaction to me to think that may be the piece of plate and the vote of thanks will be forthcoming; at the same time, unless they are both brought to a bearing in a proper manner, I would rather nothing was done at all.'

'Ye may depend on't,' said Mr. Mucklewheel, 'that it will be done very properly and in a manner to do credit both to you and the council. I'll speak to Bailie Shuttlethrift, the new Provost, to propose the thing himself, and that I'll second it.'

'Hooly, hooly,[1] friend,' quo' I, with a laugh of jocularity, no ill-pleased to see to what effect I had worked upon him; 'that will never do; ye're but a greenhorn in public affairs. The Provost maun ken nothing about it, or let on that he does na ken, which is the same thing, for folk would say that he was ettling at something of the kind for himself, and was only eager for a precedent. It would, therefore, ne'er do to speak to him. But Mr. Birky, who is to be elected into the council in my stead, would be a very proper person. For ye ken coming in as my successor, it would very naturally fall to him to speak modestly of himself, compared with me, and therefore I think he is the fittest person to make the proposal, and you, as the next youngest that has been taken in, might second the same.'

Mr. Mucklewheel agreed with me, that certainly the thing would come with the best grace from my successor.

'But I doubt,' was my answer, 'if he kens aught[2] of the matter; ye might however enquire. In short, Mr. Mucklewheel, ye see it requires a canny hand to manage public affairs, and a sound discretion to know who are the fittest to work in them. If the case were not my own, and if I was speaking for another that had done for the town what I have done, the task would be easy. For I would just rise in my place, and say as a thing of course, and admitted on all hands, "Gentlemen, it would be a very wrong thing of us, to let Mr. Mucklewheel, (that is, supposing you were me,) who has so long been a fellow-labourer with us, to quit his place here without some mark of our own esteem for him as a man, and some testimony from the council to his merits as a magistrate. Every body knows that he has been for near to fifty years a distinguished character, and has thrice filled the very highest post in the borough; that many great improvements have been made in his time, wherein his influence and wisdom was very evident; I would therefore propose, that a committee should be appointed to consider of the best means of expressing our sense of his services, in which I shall be very happy to assist, provided the Provost will consent to act as chairman."

'That's the way I would open the business, and were I the seconder, as you are to be to Mr. Birky, I would say,

"The worthy counsellor has but anticipated what every one was desirous to propose, and although a committee is a very fit way of doing the thing respectfully, there is yet a far better, and that is, for the council now sitting to come at once to a resolution on the subject, then a committee may be appointed to carry that resolution into effect."

'Having said this, you might advert first to the vote of thanks, and then to the piece of plate, to remain with the gentleman's family as a monumental testimony of the opinion which was entertained by the community of his services and character.'

Having in this judicious manner primed Mr. Mucklewheel as to the procedure, I suddenly recollected that I had a letter to write to catch the post, and having told him so, 'May be,' quo' I, 'ye would step the length of Mr. Birky's and see how he is inclined, and by the time I am done writing, ye can be back, for after all that we have been saying, and the warm and friendly interest you have taken in this business, I really would not wish my friends to stir in it, unless it is to be done in a satisfactory manner.'

Mr. Mucklewheel accordingly went to Mr. Birky, who had of course heard nothing of the subject, but they came back together, and he was very vogie[1] with the notion of making a speech before the council, for he was an upsetting[1] young man. In short, the matter was so set forward, that, on the Monday following, it was all over the town that I was to get a piece of plate at my resignation, and the whole affair proceeded so well to an issue, that the same was brought to a head to a wish. Thus had I the great satisfaction of going to my repose as a private citizen with a very handsome silver cup, bearing an inscription in the Latin tongue, of the time I had been in the council, guildry, and magistracy; and although in the outset of my public life some of my dealings may have been leavened with the leaven of antiquity, yet, upon the whole, it will not be found, I think, that, one thing weighed with another, I have been an unprofitable servant to the community. Magistrates and rulers must rule according to the maxims and affections of the world, at least whenever I tried any other way, strange obstacles started up in the opinions of men against me, and my purest intents were often more criticized than some which were less disinterested; so much is it the natural humour of mankind to jealouse and doubt the integrity of all those who are in authority and power, especially when they see them deviating from the practices of their predecessors. Posterity, therefore, or I am far mistaken, will not be angered at my plain dealing, with regard to the small motives of private advantage of which I have made mention, since it has been my endeavour to show and to acknowledge, that there is a reforming spirit abroad among men, and that really the world is gradually growing better, slowly I allow, but still it is growing better, and the main profit of the improvement will be reaped by those who are ordained to come after us.

THE END

EXPLANATORY NOTES

Abbreviations

Annals	*Annals of the Parish*, ed. James Kinsley, 1967.
Autobiography	John Galt, *Autobiography*, 2 vols., 1833.
Entail	*The Entail*, ed. Ian A. Gordon, 1970.
Minute Book	Royal Burgh of Irvine, Minutes of the Town Council (handwritten ledgers, cited by date).
Muniments	*Muniments of the Royal Burgh of Irvine*, Printed for the Ayrshire and Galloway Archaeological Association, 2 vols, Edinburgh, 1890–1.

Page 1. (1) *Gudetown*: Galt's name for his birthplace, the Royal Burgh of Irvine; an old term—cf. *Muniments*, ii. 113, which records a gift of 1702 'ffor the love and respect wee have and bear towards the good Toun of Irving'.

(2) *Writer to the Signet*: one of the ancient Scottish society of law-agents, who conducted cases before the Court of Session in Edinburgh. In Galt's novels a 'writer' is always a lawyer, never an 'author'.

(3) *beeking in the lown*: basking in the calm.

(4) *ettling*: striving.

Page 4. (1) *board*: platform on which tailors sat as they stitched.

(2) *conquest of Quebec*: 1759. Galt thus establishes the eighteenth-century setting. Pawkie is an exact contemporary of the Rev. Micah Balwhidder, whose *Annals* cover the years 1760–1810.

(3) *Cross ... Tolbooth*: The Market Cross and the 'Town House' or Tolbooth, both later demolished, were in the wide High Street. Pawkie's first shop, modest compared with his later one, was at the corner of High Street and the narrow Kirk Gate.

(4) *Irville*: Galt's alternative fictional name for Irvine.

(5) *clok*: hatch.

(6) *coothy*: affable.

Page 5. (1) *bawbee*: small coin.

(2) *a thought ajee*: somewhat slanted.

(3) *KITHING*: appearance in proper character, in one's true colours.

(4) *uncos*: (n.pl.) unusual events.

Page 6. (1) *deacon Covener*: chairman of the trade guilds. 'Deacon Con-veener of the Trades of Irvine', *Muniments* (1757 entry), ii. 141. One of the two Trades representatives on the Town Council. See Introduction, p. xiii.

(2) *the guildry*: the trade guilds (or 'Trades').

(3) *cannily*: prudently.

(4) *cod*: cushion.

(5) *mim*: prim.

(6) *ettling at*: aspiring to.

(7) *maun ca' canny*: must 'drive softly', go easy.

(8) *gleg old carlin*: sharp-witted old lady.

Page 7. (1) *redde*: advise.

(2) *friend*: close relative (here, 'husband').

(3) *fleeched*: coaxed.

(4) *greenan for*: yearning for.

(5) *barming*: fermenting.

(6) *DIRGIE*: funeral feast; from *dirige*, initial word in Latin Office of the Dead.

(7) *blateness*: bashfulness.

Page 8. (1) *deacon*: elected chairman of a trade guild.

(2) *ettling at*: aspiring to.

(3) *jooking and wising*: ducking and pushing; *to wise*: to direct.

Page 9. (1) *brae*: hill.

Page 10. (1) *infœftment*: legal possession (Scots law).

(2) *Dean of Guild*: This office on the Town Council ranked after the Provost and the two bailies.

(3) *intromit*: to have pecuniary dealings (Scots law).

(4) *tacks*: leases.

(5) *jealoused*: suspected.

(6) *their loofs creeshed*: their palms greased.

(7) *grassum*: properly, 'initial down-payment'; here, 'bribe'.

(8) *wised*: directed.

(9) *between dinner and tea-time*: dinner in the mid-eighteenth century was eaten in the early afternoon.

Page 11. (1) *crown of the causey*: raised middle of the High Street, the only part paved at this date. See chapter xv.

(2) *Whar*: where.

(3) *looting*: stooping.

(4) *thir*: (dem.pl.) these; 'news' is plural here.

(5) *election*: Members of Parliament for each group of Scottish burghs

were at this period elected by delegates appointed by the Town Councils. Cf. W. Croft Dickinson, *John Galt, 'The Provost' and the Burgh*, Greenock, 1954, p. 11. Pawkie plans to move M'Lucre up (and out) by having him appointed delegate.

(6) *spear*: ask, inquire.

(7) *the Earl*: the greatest landowner in the district, with a Castle near Irvine and a residence in London. Pawkie and he will later become close allies. Eglinton Castle, the seat of the Earl of Eglinton, Galt's model, was some two miles north of Irvine.

Page 12. (1) *half-door*: the outer door of the shop was divided into separate upper and lower 'half-doors'.

(2) *Michaelmas*: 29 September. 'They elect their magistrats viz. the provost and tuo baillies, yearly, the first Munday after Michalmas' (*Muniments*, ii. 131).

(3) *the magistracy*: the offices of provost and bailies.

(4) *swithered*: hesitated in perplexity.

Page 13. (1) *a Michaelmas mare*: a magistrate failing to get re-elected at Michaelmas.

(2) *belyve*: soon, quickly.

(3) *fashious*: troublesome.

(4) *sough*: noise (as of the wind or the sea); hence, 'rumour'.

(5) *bir*: force.

Page 14. (1) *gie*: give.

(2) *fleeching*: coaxing.

(3) *Nabob*: The Scot, returning wealthy from India, is a recurring character-type in Galt. Cf. Mr. Rupees in *The Last of the Lairds* and the successful hero of *The Member*, which—like *The Provost*—is a shrewd study of political power.

Page 15. (1) *on my Lord's side*: the Earl supported the sitting member.

(2) *crooket the snek*: bent the latch.

(3) *banned*: cursed.

(4) *this device*: Galt is drawing on an actual incident in the Town Council of 1757, when at 'the last election' a 'riot' was committed 'in carrying off by force some of our members'; *Minute Book*, 5 Feb. 1757. There had been an earlier incident, when a Councillor was 'violentlie detained' from an election by the then Dean of Guild; *Muniments* (25 Sept. 1702 entry), ii. 122.

(5) *siee tod*: sly fox.

Page 16. (1) *back rig*: A. F. McJannet, *Royal Burgh of Irvine*, Glasgow, 1938, reproduces a map of Irvine (*c.* 1820—the end of the 'period' of *The*

Provost) which shows several 'Back Riggs'—areas of cultivated ground on the burgh's perimeter.

(2) *roup*: auction.

(3) *three guineas the peck*: The 'peck' was a dry measure of capacity, varying with the district and the commodity. The Ayrshire peck of potatoes was about thirty pounds, and the price was manifest bribery.

(4) *prin-cods*: pin-cushions. They were 'stuffed' with money.

(5) *jookerie*: deceit.

(6) *bodie*: Galt's usual spelling for the sense 'person' (≠ 'body').

(7) *an o'er-sea merchant*: Irvine was in the eighteenth century a significant sea-port.

Page 17. (1) *rookit of every plack*: stripped of every penny.

(2) *the divor's bill*: the bankrupt's Act.

(3) *steading*: piece of land. This is the usual sense in *The Provost*. The word can also mean buildings (esp. farm) on the land.

(4) *the town-head*: the southern end of the eighteenth-century High Street, the limit of the built-up area. The term is still used of this part, though building has extended well beyond it. The northern end of the burgh was called 'Town's End'.

Page 18. (1) *kimmers*: companions (used of females only).

(2) *siller*: 'silver', money.

(3) *cutty-spoon*: a spoon carved from horn (and so of little value).

(4) *sprose*: ostentatious speech.

(5) *hooly*: slowly.

Page 19. (1) *notour*: notorious.

(2) *slockening*: quenching (of thirst).

(3) *gardevin*: whisky jar.

(4) *gar*: cause.

(5) *howf*: snug shelter.

Page 20. (1) *bairns' part o' geer*: children's share of (inherited) property.

(2) *bardy*: pert.

(3) *speer't*: inquired.

(4) *lowered his birsses*: (animal metaphor) 'lowered his bristles', quietened down.

(5) *trance*: Galt—ironically—has M'Lucre describe the Nabob's impressive reception hall by the term for the narrow corridor in a small Scottish house.

(6) *jookit*: dodged, avoided.

(7) *a hantle*: a fair amount.

(8) *glammer*: spell-binding speech.

Page 21. (1) *no worth ... aught*: not worth the down-payment for a new lease of the worst land in the town's possession.

(2) *my eyne maun*: my eyes must.

(3) *my ends and my awls*: (from shoe-making) 'my bits and pieces'.

Page 22. (1) *stramash*: uproar.

(2) *taking the door on my back*: (colloquial) 'leaving abruptly'.

(3) *Fly*: 'A stage-coach, distinguished by this name, in order to impress a belief in its extraordinary quickness in travelling', Johnson's *Dictionary*.

(4) *leet*: list (of candidates for a position).

Page 23. (1) *smeddum*: vigour.

(2) *sorning*: sponging.

(3) *fasherie*: trouble.

(4) *cess*: tax.

Page 24. (1) *eydent*: diligent.

(2) *Gardevin*: see p. 19, note (3).

(3) *tavert*: stupefied.

(4) *sib*: related.

(5) *groosy and oozy and doozy*: fat and slovenly and decayed.

(6) *laft*: 'loft' (the gallery of the church).

(7) *English Divine*: Galt's sly and ironical comment on the ignorance of the Town Councillors. Mr. Pittle is called to a presbyterian pulpit on the basis of an Anglican sermon by Isaac Barrow (1630–77).

Page 25. (1) *infeoffment*: legal possession (Scots law).

Page 26. (1) *braw*: 'brave', fine.

(2) *Chronicle of Dalmailing*: A typical Galt cross-reference. See *Annals*, p. 5.

(3) *clash of glar*: fistful of mud.

(4) *friend*: close relative.

Page 27. (1) *whins*: gorse-bushes.

(2) *the crooser*: the more boldly.

(3) *'bailie*: Pawkie leaves the lucrative office of Dean of Guild for the more powerful position of bailie, with the functions of a magistrate.

Page 28. (1) *donsie*: saucy.

(2) *gie no name to her gets*: give no name to her (bastard) children.

(3) *callan*: lad.

(4) *outgait and blether in the causey*: self-display and gossip in the street.

(5) *precognition*: (Scots law) preliminary examination before a magistrate to determine if there is ground for a trial at a higher court.

(6) *Tolbooth*: it contained both the Town Council offices and the jail.

(7) *lords . . . Ayr*: the Lords of Session (judges) from Edinburgh, who would preside over a murder trial at Ayr, the County Town.

Page 29. (1) *Lord Advocate*: principal law-officer of the Crown in Scotland.

(2) *wud*: mad, incensed.

(3) *Flander's baby*: 'a wooden doll produced in the Netherlands' (Webster).

(4) *by herself*: insane, out of her mind.

Page 30. (1) *misleart tinkler*: unmannerly vagrant.

(2) *martyrs in the . . . persecution*: i.e. covenanters in the late seventeenth century; cf. *Ringan Gilhaize*.

(3) *Tron*: public weighing-place, in the High Street on the north side of the Tolbooth.

(4) *our body*: i.e. the Town Council. Gimblet was one of the two members elected by the 'Trades'. Galt, as usual, carefully distinguishes between 'body' (as here) and 'bodie' (person), a distinction lost in later reprints of his work.

(5) *ee*: eye.

Page 31. (1) *we*: Pawkie is in the execution party. The junior bailie was compelled by law to attend and—if necessity arose—to complete the execution. Galt's unobtrusive accuracy of detail never wavers.

(2) *choppin*: quart.

(3) *reset*: crime of receiving stolen goods (Scots law).

Page 32. (1) *coals for a bonfire*: as Pawkie says, 'an ancient custom'. The burgh accounts for 30 May 1681 include 'ten loads of coalls furnished . . . upon the publick account of this burgh quhilk were burnt upon the 29 May' (*Muniments*, ii. 295).

(2) *wyte*: blame.

Page 33. (1) *clanjamphry*: worthless.

(2) *misleart*: unmannerly.

(3) *fashed*: troubled.

Page 34. (1) *town-officers with their halberts*: uniformed halbert-bearing town-officers still form a ceremonial guard on formal occasions in some Scottish towns, including Irvine.

(2) *His Majesty's health was drank*: This ceremonial of the Town Council drinking his Majesty's health at the public expense was quite moderate by earlier standards. On 14 Oct. 1686 'the Magistrates and Council and several gentlemen' pledged His Majesty's health in 55 pints of wine, three and a half gallons of ale, six ounces of tobacco, three and a half dozen tobacco pipes, and 'six baikis' (*Muniments*, ii. 310–11). Pawkie,

a good politician, will introduce further moderation to suit the changing times. See ch. xliii.

(3) *couped*: overturned.

(4) *Mr. Keelivine, the town-clerk*: His lawyer parent, 'father of the celebrated town-clerk of Gudetown', will appear in *The Entail*, p. 30, a typical Galt cross-link from novel to novel.

Page 35. (1) *the fire-drum*: the town-drummer, a minor officer of the Town Council, had various drum-beats in his repertoire, including an alarm for fire. Cf. ch. xxxiii.

Page 36. (1) *a detachment, as it was called*: Pawkie is being ironical on his own account. Four companies, from the regiment quartered in Ayr, is excessive for a 'detachment'.

(2) *the forty-five*: the Jacobite uprising of 1745.

Page 37. (1) *My Lord the next provost*: Galt's model, the Earl of Eglinton, was elected Provost of Irvine on several occasions, *Minute Book*, 5 Oct. 1761 and later dates.

(2) *brawest cleeding*: finest clothing.

(3) *deacons*: mere chairmen of the 'Trades'—and so less likely to behave well before My Lord than bailies, who were wealthy shopkeepers and merchants. Galt, like Jane Austen, had an eye (and ear) for the minutiae of social distinctions.

Page 38. (1) *out o' the bodie*: out of their wits.

(2) *wised*: directed, signed.

(3) *minted*: hinted.

(4) *stramash*: uproar.

(5) *sederunt*: session (Scots law); Lat. 'they were sitting'.

Page 39. (1) *sprose*: show.

(2) *the French*: this makes the date of the events 1778, the year of Pawkie's first term as Provost.

(3) *the Grand Monarque*: Louis XVI.

(4) *toozy*: shaggy.

(5) *sark neck*: shirt-neck.

Page 40. (1) *claught*: grasp.

(2) *jealouse*: suspect.

(3) *pannel*: person on trial (Scots law).

Page 41. (1) *fey*: crazy.

Page 42. (1) *American war*: this dates the chapter 1783.

(2) *leet*: list (of candidates).

(3) *kithe*: show an appearance.

Page 43. (1) *market-day*: the market took place in the wide High Street, in front of Pawkie's new shop (and extensive warehouse; cf. ch. xxxvii).

(2) *hobbleshaw*: hubbub, tumult.

(3) *forenent*: opposite.

(4) *skailed*: dispersed.

(5) *tinkler . . . randy*: vagrant . . . scold.

(6) *fifteen-pence a peck*: a 'peck' of meal was about nine pounds.

Page 44. (1) *corruption*: bad temper.

(2) *some ploy . . . anent a bairn*: i.e. the Kirk Session of Dalmailing had disciplined him for fathering a bastard.

(3) *neive*: first.

(4) *gait*: street. Probably Bridge Gate.

Page 45. (1) *closes*: narrow tunnel-like entries to houses and back-gardens.

(2) *skailed*: dispersed.

(3) *Lord Advocate*: principal law-officer of the Crown in Scotland, who would have the responsibility of prosecuting the offenders.

(4) *capps and luggies*: terms for wooden bowls.

Page 46. (1) *since syne*: since then, ever since.

(2) *the meal mob*: Sixteen pence a pound was dear for meal at this date. The chapter is based on an actual 'Meal Riot' in Irvine in 1777, which led the Council to authorize Councillor Hugh Galt to purchase meal and sell it at 'no more than 10½d per peck'. See *Minute Book*, 12 July 1777.

Page 47. (1) *the eighty-eight*: 1788.

(2) *sickerly*: securely.

Page 48. (1) *jookerie cookerie*: shifty manipulation. *jook*: dodge, shift aside.

(2) *outcry*: Galt bases this incident on a lease of Town Moor to 'his lordship', the Earl of Eglinton, which resulted in a petition of protest from the Trades. The petition is transcribed in *Minute Book*, 6 Aug. 1804.

Page 49. (1) *steadings*: pieces of land for building; also the buildings themselves.

(2) *lones*: (1) a narrow pathway; English 'lane': (2) pathway (as here) between house-frontages and paved middle of the street.

(3) *pavement*: the paved surface of the middle of the street.

Page 50. (1) *choppin*: quart.

(2) *greybeard*: large, earthenware bottle (also 'pig', from resemblance).

(3) *bir*: force.

(4) *inns*: inn. The plural form with singular meaning (cf. 'lodgings'),

obsolete in English, was still current in Scots and is the usual form in Galt. It is often normalized in reprints.

Page 51. (1) *Whinstone-quarry*: whinstone (basalt) quarry at Dunton Knoll, on the edge of the burgh. 'To James Galt for stones from Dunton Knoll £2.3.8' (*Muniments* (1745 entry), ii. 333).

(2) *spunkit*: sparked.

(3) *big a dyke*: build a wall. Pawkie gets a free boundary wall round his new property at the Town End. He has now extended his holdings to the north end of the town.

Page 52. (1) *lofts*: raised gallery at back of church.

(2) *edification*: i.e. 'building'.

Page 53. (1) *pews . . . became . . . a vendible property*: Three pews in the Irvine Kirk were auctioned ('rouped') for £12.10.0, £14.10.0, and £30.15.0, *Minute Book*, 15 June 1783.

Page 54. (1) *anent the bigging of a land of houses*: concerning the building of a block of flats. 'Land' is a single building, multi-storey in Glasgow and Edinburgh, probably two-storey-high in Irvine. A 'house' in a 'land' is (in modern terms) a 'flat'. Pawkie consolidates his grip on the northern end of the town.

(2) *conjuncture*: turn of events, occasion.

(3) *coothy crack*: cosy yarn.

Page 55. (1) *bigging . . . fundament*: building . . . foundation.

(2) *an unco*: a strange thing.

Page 56. (1) *Mr. Threeper, the writer*: This lawyer ('Writer to the Signet') will reappear in *The Entail*, p. 179; *threep*: argue.

(2) *cried*: called out.

Page 57. (1) *rookit*: stripped.

Page 58. (1) *pinnets*: pennants, streamers.

Page 59. (1) *brulies*: fights.

(2) *the Greenhead*: the upper end of 'the Green', by the river Garnock, at some distance from the centre of town.

Page 60. (1) *volunteers*: 'Considering the propriety and necessity of Raising Men for the Defence of the Kingdome', Irvine Town Council offered a bounty of two guineas to each volunteer (*Minute Book*, 27 March 1793).

Page 61. (1) *canny*: prudent.

(2) *loot a sort a-jee*: bend a bit sideways.

Page 62. (1) *forenent*: opposite.

(2) *Gude saves*: God save us. The *Blackwood Standard Novels* edition, ed. D. M. Moir, prints 'Gude save's'. Galt, in his manuscripts and all texts which he is known to have proofed, avoids the use of the apostrophe commonly found in nineteenth-century printing of Scots. His spelling is strictly phonetic and (notably in the spelling of present participle forms, like *greenan* for the commoner *greenin*') is etymologically sound.

(3) *sick feckless*: such feeble.

Page 63. (1) *waled*: picked, chosen.

Page 64. (1) *wise*: direct.

(2) *blate*: bashful, shy.

Page 66. (1) *Cotton Mill*: Cotton spinning was an important Irvine industry. 'Cotton works' were set up on 'some of the Town's ground' (*Minute Book*, 2 May 1792). The name 'Cotton Street' still survives.

(2) *rigs and gables*: fields and houses.

(3) *scog*: shelter (in secret).

(4) *jealousies*: suspicions.

Page 68. (1) *callan*: lad.

(2) *weans*: children.

Page 70. (1) *vacant steading*: piece of land not built on. Pawkie steadily increases his holding of property.

(2) *loyalty of the borough ... assurances to the contrary*: The Council offered a reward of three guineas to every able-bodied seaman of the Burgh 'who shall voluntarily enter himself to serve in his Majesty's Ships of Warr' (*Minute Book*, 7 July 1779).

(3) *Michaelmas dinner*: the annual dinner following the Michaelmas elections.

Page 71. (1) *gash old carl*: shrewd old fellow.

(2) *sprose*: bravado.

(3) *glammer*: enchantment.

(4) *trew*: trust, believe.

Page 72. (1) *funny weans and misleart trades-lads*: facetious children and unmannerly apprentices.

(2) *daffing*: making sport.

(3) *gavawlling*: revelling.

Page 73. (1) *caterpillar*: self-revelation in a brilliant metaphor. An Irvine town-map, marked off with the shops, houses, steadings, etc. relentlessly acquired by Pawkie, notably resembles a leaf eaten by a caterpillar.

(2) *flourishes*: (the metaphor continued) flowers.

Page 74. (1) *thir*: these.

(2) *by-hand*: underhand.

Page 75. (1) *Norawa deals*: Norway planks (of timber).

(2) *pigs from the lum-heads*: 'pigs' (so called from the resemblance) were draught-promoting caps on the chimney-tops ('lum-heads').

(3) *carry*: moving cloud.

(4) *warsling*: wrestling.

Page 76. (1) *lift*: sky.

(2) *.hirpling*: limping.

(3) *to the kirkyard, to look at the vessels*: the churchyard, in the elevated part of the town, had a clear view of the port, now lost, but in the eighteenth century jealously preserved. A tenant was granted a lease to build in the lower part of the town with a prohibition against 'erecting any building which would stop . . . the view of the shipping' (*Minute Book*, 1 Sept. 1794).

(4) *joes*: sweethearts.

(5) *lameter*: cripple.

Page 78. (1) *norit*: norward, north.

(2) *betherel*: beadle, gravedigger.

Page 79. (1) *a topping line*: a spinning business. *Top, tap*: bundle of wool or flax prepared for spinning.

(2) *mortification*: property bequeathed for charity (Scots law).

Page 80. (1) *fleeched*: coaxed.

(2) *bardy*: pert, forward.

(3) *temporality*: 'timely' assistance.

(4) *an end's errand*: (usually 'an aince errand') an errand for one specific purpose. *aince*: once.

Page 81. (1) *by common*: uncommon.

(2) *furthy*: affable, forthcoming.

(3) *quistical*: eccentric. (A coinage, blending 'queer', 'quiz', 'twist', and 'caustical'.)

(4) *pioye*: firework (made of moulded damp gun-powder).

Page 82. (1) *spunky*: 'sparky', irritable.

(2) *o'er-come*: refrain.

Page 83. (1) *kithed*: showed.

(2) *lamps*: Galt bases this incident on the 1804 decision of the Council that, if the 'inhabitants' purchased and erected lamps, 'the Magistrates and Council will aggree to defray the expenses of furnishing oil and up-holding them in time coming' (*Minute Book*, 17 Oct. 1804).

(3) *news of victory*: Peace of Amiens, 1801.

Page 84. (1) *snod*: tidy.

Page 85. (1) *plain-stones*: flagged pavement.

(2) *loans*: See ch. xv.

(3) *syvers*: gutters, drains.

(4) *ronns*: gutters on roof to carry off rainwater, down-pipes.

(5) *nepus-gables*: small gables, with a roof projecting from the main roof of a house.

Page 86. (1) *the plain-stones of Glasgow*: cf. *The Entail*, pp. 277, 406.

(2) *kepp*: intercept (and so channel).

(3) *fasherie*: trouble.

(4) *grassum*: payment, bribe.

(5) *villa-house*: house of some pretension.

(6) *change-house*: inn (originally one where a change of horses was available).

(7) *bardy*: impudent.

(8) *soop her flags*: sweep her paving-stones.

Page 87. (1) *cloyt*: heavy fall.

(2) *prejink*: precise (in manner or dress).

(3) *by herself*: crazy, out of her mind.

(4) *offended the law*: 'Some persons have met with much hurt' and the Dean of Guild was empowered to enforce the removal of 'Rubbish from the Streets' (*Minute Book*, 5 May 1794).

(5) *latheron*: sloven.

(6) *speer*: inquire, ask.

(7) *set up his birzes*: 'set up his bristles', made him angry.

Page 88. (1) *intromission*: transaction (Scots law).

(2) *second edition of the late war*: 1803.

Page 89. (1) *wakerife*: wakeful.

(2) *arles*: earnests.

(3) *Lord-lieutenant*: peer (or major land-owner) appointed by Sovereign as chief executive of a County. 'My Lord' (resident in London) was both Lord-lieutenant and frequently Provost and so a doubly useful ally of Pawkie.

Page 93. (1) *Duke of York*: as commander-in-chief introduced army reforms in the early nineteenth century.

(2) *galravitching*: disorderly.

(3) *fou*: 'full', drunk.

Page 94. (1) *lave*: remainder.

(2) *cauldrife*: chilly.

(3) *jealoused*: suspected.

Page 96. (1) *my second Provostry*: 1789–91 (cf. ch. xiv).

(2) *ettling*: striving, ambitious.

Page 97. (1) *the hempies . . . jouked themselves*: the rogues . . . cheated themselves.

(2) *sillybobs*: sillabubs, flavoured drinks made with milk.

Page 98. (1) *a gi'en horse*: a gift horse; *gi'en*: given.

Page 99. (1) *kithed in evil*: resulted ('made their appearance') in damage.

Page 100. (1) *gabby prick-me-dainty bodie*: talkative, 'pernickety', person.

(2) *well dockit*: pretentious; *dock*: strut conceitedly (used only of a small person).

(3) *on chandler's pins*: 'over elegant'; literally, 'set up on candle-stick pins'. Cf. colloquial 'stuck up'.

(4) *ettling*: striving, ambitious. James Watt (1736–1819), the inventor of the first practical steam-engine, was a native of Greenock.

Page 101. (1) *wipes*: sarcastic remarks.

(2) *arles*: earnests.

(3) *stotted . . . birslet pea*: bounced out of his chair with the liveliness (spark) of a scorched pea.

(4) *oure*: 'over', too.

(5) *prejinck*: precise.

(6) *a divor bodie*: ne'er-do-well person. Irvine Burgh Council seemed to have attracted drunks as town-drummers. The 1761 drummer was compelled to 'deliver up the Town's Drum and Sticks . . . and his Livery Coat Vest and Breeches'. The 1791 drummer was discontinued 'for his Misconduct'; and the 1817 drummer was replaced since 'for a considerable time past has now been unfit for his duty' (*Minute Books*, 11 March 1761, 26 May 1791, 29 March 1817).

Page 102. (1) *plooky as a curran bun*: pimply as a currant bun.

(2) *partan's tae*: crab's claw ('toe').

(3) *wamblet*: wobbled.

(4) *skayling*: dispersing.

(5) *stramash*: tumult.

(6) *corruption*: anger.

Page 103. (1) *a new one*: Cf. 'tua skinns of pairchment . . . to be heids to the touns drum' (*Muniments* (31 May 1681 entry), ii. 295).

Page 104. (1) *change house*: tavern, inn.

(2) *the fire-beat*: a special warning tattoo.

(3) *our houses were all insured*: the plural 'houses' is ironically significant. Pawkie is by now a considerable owner of house-property.

(4) *throng*: (adj.) busy.

Page 105. (1) *cried*: shouted.
(2) *hobbleshaw*: hubbub.
(3) *oure cauld*: too ('over') cold.

Page 106. (1) *goud in goupins*: *goud*: gold. *goupin*: the amount contained in both hands held in the form of a bowl.
(2) *gausie*: jolly.
(3) *to intromit*: to have dealings (Scots law).
(4) *Bodle*: a 'cross-reference' to *The Entail* (still unwritten), p. 78 etc.

Page 107. (1) *cuts and copper-plates*: i.e. an illustrated edition of Richardson's *Clarissa Harlowe*.
(2) *antiquity and lappets*: old-fashioned dress and streamers hanging from headgear.

Page 108. (1) *ruth*: compassionate.
(2) *far ben*: very intimate. *ben*: inner room of a small Scottish house.
(3) *ajee*: ajar, open.

Page 109. (1) *glaik*: gleam.
(2) *The Theatre Royal*: Irvine had no theatre, only Mr. Dribble's barn, which Galt dignifies by the title of the Greenock theatre, where in 1818 he had seen his play *The Appeal* performed by a similar travelling company.

Page 110. (1) *ring*: 'reign', dominate.
(2) *doited*: crazed.

Page 111. (1) *ramplor*: gay and rambling, 'rampageous'.
(2) *randy*: disorderly.
(3) *latheron*: sloven.

Page 112. (1) *order the players to decamp*: This incident provided the theme for Sir David Wilkie's painting, *The Parish Beadle* (1822), where a town officer is depicted arresting players, including a 'termagant woman'. Galt, aware of their parallel interests in Scottish small-town scenes, had earlier provided Wilkie with the theme for the painting *The Penny Wedding*. For Galt's letter to Wilkie 12 May 1807 (Nat. Lib. Scot. MS. 9835, ff. 15–16) see I. A. Gordon, *John Galt*, 1972, pp. 10–11.
(2) *flit her howff*: shift her refuge.

Page 113. (1) *between the tyning and the winning*: 'between the losing and the winning'. Proverbial phrase meaning 'on the balance between two choices of conduct'.
(2) *funny*: mocking.
(3) *spunk*: spark.

Page 114. (1) *hobbleshow*: hubbub.

Page 115. (1) *an ignominious end*: the death penalty for duelling.

(2) *yett*: gate.

(3) *stang*: 'sting', shock.

Page 116. (1) *thir twa three pounds*: these few (two or three) pounds.

(2) *when he was out of his time, as a writer*: when he had completed his training, as a lawyer.

Page 117. (1) *INTERLOCUTOR*: judgment of the court (Scots law).

(2) *kent-speckle*: conspicuous.

(3) *gavaulling*: revelry.

(4) *prejink*: precise.

(5) *public washing-house on the Green*: this public utility, according to the *Minute Books*, was prudently leased by the Council to a 'tacksman'.

Page 118. (1) *boyne*: tub.

(2) *haverelling*: fooling.

(3) *pig*: earthenware jar (from resemblance).

(4) *hilt or hair*: (prov.) 'not a trace'; hilt: *flesh*.

(5) *latheron*: sloven.

Page 119. (1) *the Cross-well*: water was available only from public wells. The well at the Cross served the busy High Street, with its houses, shops, and market. In 1834 there was a petition 'for a new or additional well near the Cross' (*Minute Book*, 13 Oct. 1834).

(2) *tod*: fox.

Page 120. (1) *bardy*: impudent.

(2) *owre het*: too hot.

Page 121. (1) *coom*: dirt.

(2) *lear*: learning.

(3) *ettering*: festering.

(4) *writer*: lawyer.

(5) *Lords*: law lords (judges).

Page 122. (1) *read essays, and debate*: Galt recalls the Society (cf. *Autobiography*) he founded at the same age—but he views it through Pawkie's older eyes. See I. A. Gordon, *John Galt*, 1972, p. 8.

(2) *deacon*: expert.

(3) *neither bir nor smeddum*: neither force nor spirit.

Page 123. (1) *stot*: bounce.

(2) *canny wising*: prudent directing.

(3) *kithed*: showed.

Page 124. (1) *keeking*: prying.

(2) *the good plain old places*: these were (1) the Grammar School,

offering Latin and Greek, (2) the 'English School of the Burgh of Irvine'.
Rivalry between their respective headmasters (see *Muniments*, ii. 145) is
Galt's starting-point for this chapter.

Page 125. (1) *a beautiful academy*: The Council approved the foundation
of an Academy—with a rector—about this time (*Minute Book*, 23 Oct.
1813).

(2) *big*: build.

(3) *my new steading, at the Westergate*: Pawkie, for all his 'reformed'
ways, continues his 'caterpillar' consumption of the town. Having spread
south and north, he now moves west. Westergate (West Backway) was on
the edge of the Burgh towards the open public Green.

Page 126. (1) *thole*: endure.

(2) *fashed*: toubled.

(3) *fozy*: 'mushy', inflated.

(4) *the Ayr Bank*: a local, disastrous, banking venture; founded 1769,
suspended payments 1772. Cf. *The Entail*, p. 42.

(5) *the English teacher*: headmaster of 'the English School'. See p. 124,
note (2).

Page 127. (1) *hale and hearty, not exceeding three score and seven*: a
comment in character by the indestructible Pawkie, who (on Galt's always
meticulous chronology) was himself now well in his seventies.

Page 128. (1) *peutering*: canvassing for votes.

(2) *delegate*: see p. 11, note (5).

Page 129. (1) *Britannia in a picture*: Thomas Gilray did many allegorical
engravings with Britannia as the centre figure.

(2) *tak' tent*: take care.

Page 130. (1) *upsetting*: ambitious.

Page 131. (1) *vogie*: cheerful.

(2) *gauger*: exciseman.

(3) *forbye*: apart from.

Page 132. (1) *the rebuilding of the Cross-well*: See p. 119, note (1).

Page 133. (1) *crouse and vogie*: confident and cheerful.

(2) *grippy*: greedy, grasping. Galt's next novel, *The Entail*, was to be
subtitled 'The Lairds of Grippy'.

Page 134. (1) *galravitch both at hack and manger*: 'guzzle freely', riot, like
an animal with free access to the hack (hayrack). For the cost of earlier
'galravitchings' see p. 34, note (2).

(2) *gavaulling*: rioting.

(3) *one of the . . . sederunts*: one of the most certain (drinkers) of all the former sessions.

Page 135. (1) *friend*: relation.
(2) *by common*: out of the usual.

Page 136. (1) *jealouse*: suspect.
(2) *mumpileese*: perhaps 'monopolise'. But Mr. Peevie's inflated jargon and malapropisms are not intended to be accurately understood.

Page 137. (1) *to cleek and oxter him*: to support him by a hold ('cleek') under his armpit ('oxter').
(2) *cagie*: sportive.

Page 138. (1) *the abbreviation I had made of the Michaelmas galravitching*: Pawkie's change of heart was founded on an actual decision of the Burgh Council 'to discontinue the former practice of giving public entertainment' (*Minute Book*, 21 April 1820).

Page 139. (1) *the new bridge . . . and the toll thereon*: the bridge, linking the port with the town, was a toll point and an important part of the town's revenue.
(2) *Peace came round, and our prosperity began to fall off*: Galt (like Pawkie) took a realistic view. In 1812, when Wellington's success in Spain deprived him of a lucrative agency, he noted candidly 'I repined at his victories'. See Ian A. Gordon, *John Galt*, pp. 14–16.

Page 140. (1) *STRAMASH*: uproar.

Page 141. (1) *neeves*: fists.
(2) *the Fifteen at Edinburgh*: the fifteen Lords of Session (judges).

Page 142. (1) *girn*: snare, 'grin' (*dial* and *obs. O.E.D.*).
(2) *bir*: force.

Page 143. (1) *wuddy*: noose.

Page 144. (1) *longer-nebbit and more kittle*: longer nosed and more difficult.

Page 145. (1) *callants*: lads.
(2) *lay your hairs in the water*: 'go fishing' (boys caught fish with a horse-hair noose).

Page 147. (1) *feued*: leased for a ground-rent.
(2) *supply of water by pipes*: in place of the public wells of the earlier period.
(3) *their*: these (usually 'thir').
(4) *outgate*: outlet, escape.

(5) *the cloth shop and wine cellar*: the first mention of Pawkie's second business, but implicitly of long standing.

Page 148. (1) *ettled*: striven.
(2) *peutering*: canvassing (for favours).

Page 149. (1) *birzing*: 'bruising', crushing.

Page 150. (1) *Hooly*: slowly.
(2) *kens aught*: knows anything.

Page 151. (1) *vogie*: pleased.

Page 152. (1) *upsetting*: ambitious.